★

Yasmine thought she spotted a familiar baseball cap inside the coffee shop. *Please let him be alone,* she thought.

Hank was sitting at one of the front booths. He had an enormous glass of soda in front of him. He was laughing, which made Yasmine think he probably wasn't alone. Some of his friends must have been seated on the other side of the booth.

Yasmine couldn't see them. But then she heard Yago's voice. "Okay, Hank, your turn, buddy-boy!"

Hank gulped down about half his soda. Then he started burping the national anthem! He got all the way to "what so proudly we hailed" before he ran out of air.

Yasmine froze, too grossed out to move. Did she really want people to think she liked this guy? What if he started burping songs at her friends?

She shuddered and backed out of the coffee shop practically on tiptoe. *Forget Hank,* she told herself when she was safely back in the lobby. *In fact, forget boys—at least until you're twenty-one. Or thirty-one.*

Tournament Trouble

Tournament
Trouble

by

Emily Costello

A SKYLARK BOOK
NEW YORK · TORONTO · LONDON · SYDNEY · AUCKLAND

RL 5, 008–012

TOURNAMENT TROUBLE

A Bantam Skylark Book/January 1999

Skylark Books is a registered trademark of Bantam Books, a division of Bantam Doubleday Dell Publishing Group, Inc. Registered in U.S. Patent and Trademark Office and elsewhere.

ISBN 0-553-48649-7

Published simultaneously in the United States and Canada

Bantam Books are published by Bantam Books, a division of Bantam Doubleday Dell Publishing Group, Inc. Its trademark, consisting of the words "Bantam Books" and the portrayal of a rooster, is Registered in U.S. Patent and Trademark Office and in other countries. Marca Registrada. Bantam Books, 1540 Broadway, New York, New York 10036.

PRINTED IN THE UNITED STATES OF AMERICA

OPM   0   9   8   7   6   5   4   3   2   1

For my editor, Diana Capriotti,
who plays with heart and humor

chapter 1

"Yo, Geena!" Tess Adams called. "Heads up!"

Geena Di Gregorio looked up just in time to see a soccer ball whizzing straight toward her. She stepped forward and stuck out her chest. Pulling in her rib cage, she let the ball drop to her feet.

The Stars—Geena's American Youth Soccer Organization, or AYSO, team—were gathered at the Beachside playing fields. It was the Thursday before Columbus Day weekend, school was closed for the holiday, and they were getting ready to leave for the Midwestern Shootout, a big tournament outside Chicago. Everyone was excited and full of energy.

"Geena!" Yasmine Madrigal hollered. "Over here!"

Geena dribbled around her suitcases and pushed the ball toward Yasmine.

"Nice pass!" Nicole Philips-Smith called.

Geena felt her face flush with pleasure. It *had* been a nice pass. *I couldn't have done that last season,* she told herself. Playing with the Stars had really improved her soccer skills.

Which is a nice side benefit, Geena thought. She was more excited about the new friends she had made on the team.

Nicole and Geena were best friends. And Geena felt close to Tess, Tameka Thomas, Yasmine, Fiona Fagan, and Lacey Essex—girls who had been on her team two seasons in a row now.

Four other players had just joined the team that season. Geena liked the new Stars too.

Yardley Gallagher made her laugh. Yard played the way Geena had played when she'd first started—terribly. But she had a sense of humor about her lack of ability.

Kyoto Funaki was a great dresser, and Geena was hoping to learn a thing or two from her about handling the ball.

The other two new girls on the team, Rory Carver and Sheila McGarth, weren't as nice. But since they were Geena's teammates, she was trying to make friends with them, too.

Yasmine stopped the ball. She stuck the toe of her shoe underneath it and sent it into the air. Yasmine caught the ball on one knee. She juggled it knee to knee a few times and then power-kicked it to Tess.

"Beautiful!" Geena called.

"Hey! Tameka and Mr. Thomas are here," Lacey called. She pointed to the parking lot. A big gray van, driven by Tameka's father, the Stars' head coach, had just pulled in. Mr. Thomas had rented the van to take the team to the tournament. "Let's go!"

Geena grabbed her bags. She hurried over to the van with Nicole and the rest of the team.

"Let's sit here," Nicole said, sliding into the middle seat.

Geena sat next to Nicole. She put her bags down with a relieved sigh.

"Three bags?" Nicole said. "We're only going to be gone for four days. What all did you bring?"

Geena nudged a blue bag with her foot. "In this one, I've got soda, potato chips, corn chips, pretzels, apples, pears, grapes."

Tess leaned forward from the seat behind them. "Didn't you pack any *clothes*?" she asked.

Geena nudged a red bag. "Sure. I've got a separate bag for that."

Nicole peered under the seat. "What's in the backpack?"

"My camera, a couple of packs of cards, some other games, last month's *Fourteen* magazine—"

"Can I see the *Fourteen*?" Tameka asked.

"Sure." Geena pulled the magazine out and passed it over Nicole's lap to Tameka, who was sitting next to the window.

"Do you have a chess set in there?" Tess asked with a laugh.

"Yeah," Geena said happily. "I packed one just for you." Tess loved to play chess—a fact Geena had a hard time absorbing. Tess was so into soccer that it was difficult to imagine she had other interests as well. Apparently, she was also a straight-A student.

"You really thought of everything," Tess said.

"She started packing weeks ago," Nicole reported.

"I wanted to make sure the whole team had a great time," Geena explained.

"You should be our team social director during the tournament," Nicole said.

Geena smiled. The team would be together twenty-four hours a day for the next four days and nights. "Just leave it to me," she told the others. "I'll turn this tournament into one long party."

Tess sat back and stared out the van window. The sun was just going down. She watched the backs of houses flashing by.

Every mile takes us closer to Chicago, she thought with growing excitement.

Tess got to play soccer with the Stars three hours each week. She spent an extra couple of hours playing in her backyard. But even that wasn't enough. She felt as if she could play *thirty* hours and never get sick of the game.

But for the next four days, Tess would have plenty of opportunity to play. Four whole days of soccer— what could be better?

"Yippee!" Yasmine cheered when Mr. Thomas pulled into the parking lot of the Shoreline Hotel at a little after seven o'clock. They'd been in the van for over an hour and her legs were ready for a stretch.

"Look!" Kyoto said as they drove down the hotel's driveway. She pointed at a sign that said WELCOME BEACHSIDE AYSO!

"Is that just for us?" Mrs. Essex, Lacey's mother and the team's assistant coach, asked from the passenger seat.

"Nope," Mr. Thomas told her. "A couple of other teams from our league are staying here too."

"Yeah, like the Suns." Yasmine made a face at Kyoto, who was sitting next to her.

Kyoto had only been a Star for a few weeks. But Yasmine had already told her that her twin brother, Yago, was a big pain.

"Don't worry," Kyoto told Yasmine with a laugh. "I'll protect you from your brother."

"Thanks," Yasmine said.

Mr. Thomas pulled under the canopy in front of the hotel's front entrance. Yaz pulled open the van's sliding passenger door. She grabbed her overnight bag and hopped out. She waited while the rest of the Stars got their stuff organized.

A moment later a van almost identical to the Stars' nosed under the canopy and stopped. Yaz felt her stomach tighten when the van's door opened and her twin brother's familiar figure appeared. Yago was chomping on a piece of gum. His long skinny legs stuck out of a pair of shorts, and he was wearing tube socks without shoes.

"Hey, Spazz!" Yago called, waving.

Yasmine turned away. Her friends called her Yaz. But Yago always pretended her nickname was Spazz. She hated that.

Even with her back turned, Yasmine could hear Yago and his teammates clowning around. They were making pretend farting noises. At least she *hoped* they were pretend ones.

Lacey climbed out of the van, spotted the boys, and broke into a big smile. "The Suns are staying here too? Cool!" She raised her voice and shouted, "Hi, Yago!"

"Shhh," Yasmine whispered. "Please don't make him come over here."

Lacey sighed heavily. "Oh, all right."

Yasmine didn't understand why Lacey insisted on flirting with Yago. She already had a sort-of boyfriend, Cole. But Lacey was always saying how cute Yago was.

In Yasmine's opinion, Yago was about as cute as

a four-foot rat. Unlike Lacey and most of the other Stars, Yasmine wasn't boy crazy. What was there to be crazy about? Yago and his friends acted as if they were about twelve *weeks*—not twelve years—old. *Immature* didn't even begin to describe the way they behaved.

When Yago's friends came over to the Madrigals' house, they spent entire days reading comic books and playing computer games. They ate peanut-butter-and-potato-chip sandwiches and slurped milk from the carton. They left their dishes all over the family room.

Yago and his pals loved to torture Yasmine. They hid her schoolbooks and left plastic vomit in her underwear drawer. Once, they'd even turned all the furniture in her bedroom upside down.

"Hey, Yaz!" Tameka called. "Are you coming? Dad wants to see all of us in the lobby. He's going to give us our keys."

"Coming," Yasmine said, hurrying toward her friends. She couldn't wait to get into her room. Yago and his friends couldn't bother her there.

WHOA! TESS THOUGHT AS SHE WALKED INTO the hotel lobby. The place was chaotic. A constant stream of kids and coaches moved through the large, low-ceilinged room.

Mrs. Essex motioned the Stars toward a small sitting area. "Let's wait over here, out of the way," she called.

Tess dropped her bag next to the love seat where Mrs. Essex sat down. She checked out the scene while they waited for Mr. Thomas to come back.

The entire hotel seemed to be filled with soccer kids and their coaches. They were milling around the gift shop and the coffee shop—both of which were just off the lobby. Some of the kids were wearing MIDWESTERN SHOOTOUT shirts with a cartoon of a Wild West cowboy holding a soccer ball.

Tess loved the atmosphere. A whole hotel full of soccer freaks! How cool was that?

Mr. Thomas came over to the group. "Okay, everyone. Listen up. These cards will let you into your rooms."

He gave each girl something that looked like a credit card. Tess examined hers. The card had holes punched in it.

"Please pass these tournament schedules around," Mr. Thomas went on, handing Sheila a stack of bright pink papers. "As you can see, the opening ceremony is tomorrow morning at nine o'clock. We have a game immediately following that, starting at ten-thirty. Breakfast will be available in the banquet room off the lobby starting at seven. I want you to be ready to leave the hotel and head for the playing fields at eight-fifteen."

Tess took the schedules from Sheila, kept one, and passed them on to Yardley. She glanced at hers briefly. One event caught her eye. The next evening there would be a pizza party with a "mystery guest." That sounded intriguing.

"In case you need anything, I'm in room number 544," Mr. Thomas was saying when Tess tuned back in. "Mrs. Essex is in 712. Now, neither of us wants to spend the next four days checking up on you girls. We'll assume that you're mature enough to behave like grown-ups. All that will change, however, the moment I hear even a *rumor* that one of you is creating a problem of any kind. Understand?"

"Yes," Tess mumbled along with the rest of the team.

"Mrs. Essex and I expect you to check in with us at mealtimes and each night before bed," Mr. Thomas continued. "Now why don't you go up and put your stuff in your rooms? Give me a call if there are any problems."

Tess was sharing a room with Tameka, Yaz, and Kyoto. The girls picked up their gear and hauled it over to the elevators. They rode up to the fifth floor and found their room. Tess slipped the key card into a little slot. The door popped open.

"Groovy," Kyoto said.

Tess nodded as she walked in. The room had two big beds covered with patterned bedspreads. Tess dropped her stuff on the floor next to one. The TV sat on a low bureau, the remote control neatly placed on top.

"Are there any good channels?" Tameka asked, flicking on the set.

The telephone on the nightstand began to ring.

Yasmine made a face. "That's probably my mom, calling to check on me."

Tess smiled. Mrs. Madrigal was very protective of Yaz and Yago. Tess's own mother was totally different. When Tess had told her about the tournament, Mrs. Adams had said she would spend the long weekend working at her real estate office. Tess didn't expect to talk to her until she got home.

Yasmine leaned over and scooped up the phone on the second ring. "Hello? Hi, Geena. Good idea! We'll be right up."

"What did Geena want?" Tameka asked.

"Party in room 707!" Yaz announced.

"Cool!" Tameka turned off the TV. "Let's go."

Tess pocketed her key card and followed the others into the hallway. They took the elevator up two flights and knocked on the door of room 707. Geena let them in. She was sharing the room with Nicole, Lacey, and Fiona.

Geena had piled all the snacks she'd brought on the bureau. Tess wandered over and helped herself to a handful of pretzels.

Lacey was painting Nicole's fingernails a yellow that matched the Stars' uniforms.

"Can I be next?" Yasmine asked.

"Sure," Lacey said.

Someone knocked on the door, and Geena let Yardley in.

"Where are Sheila and Rory?" Tess asked. Yard was sharing a room with them.

"They hooked up with one of their friends from school," Yard said. "I don't think we're going to see much of them—except at games and official stuff."

Tess shrugged. She couldn't blame Sheila and Rory if they didn't want to hang out with the Stars. Nicole had an old feud with Sheila, and had done everything possible to make them feel unwelcome.

"Hey! Here's a movie that's just starting," Nicole announced, nodding toward the television.

This movie is pretty good, Tess thought later, as

the story developed. It was about a summer camp that was haunted by the ghost of a kid who'd died in a boating accident. One scene even took place on the camp's soccer field.

"So, Tess," Lacey said during one of the commercial breaks. "Who do you think the special guest is going to be tomorrow night?"

"Cobi Jones," Tameka answered.

"Yes!" Kyoto gave her a high five. They were both big Cobi fans. Tameka even wore her hair in tiny braids because they looked like Cobi's dreadlocks.

"Meeting Cobi would be cool," Tess said. "But personally, I'm hoping for Mia Hamm."

"Who's she?" Yardley asked.

"A member of the U.S. National Team," Tess said. "Plays attacker. She was a three-time All-American when she was in college at the University of North Carolina. She played on the Olympic squad that won a gold medal at the Atlanta Games."

"All right, all right!" Yard said. "I get the idea. She's a total soccer goddess."

Tess nodded. "Mia Hamm is probably the best soccer player in the world."

"Shhh," Nicole said. "The movie is coming back on."

When the credits began to roll at the end of the movie, Nicole picked up the remote and started channel surfing. "What's on now?" she asked.

Tess glanced at her watch: 9:57. At home she usually went to bed at nine.

"This looks good," Tameka told Nicole.

Nicole stopped on a medical drama. A woman dressed in nurse's whites was pushing a gurney down a long corridor and shouting for help.

"Guts and Glory!" Fiona said enthusiastically. "I never get to watch this show at home. It comes on just as I'm going up to bed."

Tess looked at her teammates. Lacey was yawning, and she saw Kyoto rub her eyes. Most of the girls were staring blankly at the TV. Only Geena still looked wide-awake.

"I think I'll go downstairs and hit the sack," Tess said. She stood up and stretched.

"Already?" Geena asked. "It's only ten o'clock!"

"Well, it's past my usual bedtime," Tess explained. "And we have to be up by seven-thirty tomorrow. I just want to be sure I'm alert for the game."

Tameka got up. "I'll come downstairs with you," she told Tess.

15

Yard had been leaning against Tameka. When Tameka moved, she was forced to sit up. "I just read this article about sleep for science class," she said. "Lack of sleep can slow your reaction time and ruin your athletic performance. Let's face it— I can't afford to lose any sleep. I already play like a zombie."

Lacey stretched out on the bed. "Good, now I have room to lie down."

Nicole flicked off the TV. "Looks like this party is over."

"But it's still *early*," Geena complained.

"I'm pooped," Kyoto told Geena. "See you in the morning."

Tess felt good as she walked with her roommates toward the elevator. She hadn't expected the rest of them to go to bed just because she did. *They care about this tournament as much as I do,* Tess thought happily as she pushed the Down button.

She couldn't help feeling as though she were partly responsible. When she'd joined the Stars, her teammates hadn't cared about anything except having a good time. Now they seemed to realize that playing well was important too.

★

"You guys are such a bunch of wimps," Geena grumbled as she picked up the dirty cups and empty food wrappers the other Stars had left behind. "Here we are, all together at a great hotel, and what do you want to do? Sleep."

"We can talk for a while after we get in bed," Lacey suggested. She was standing in front of the mirror, brushing her hair.

"It's not the same," Geena complained.

Fiona had already curled up under the covers. "What do you have against sleeping, anyway?"

"Nothing!" Geena said. "I just don't understand why you guys can't sleep at home. The next few nights are our big chance to have a good time."

Nicole crawled into bed. A moment later Lacey finished with her hair and snuggled under the covers too.

Geena turned in a circle. The room was neat. She didn't have any excuse not to get into bed. In truth, she *was* a little tired. But she refused to let her roommates know that.

"Would you turn off the light, Geena?" Fiona asked.

"Sure," Geena said with a dramatic sigh. "But I expect you guys to be more fun tomorrow. We have to stay up *at least* until midnight."

★

Yasmine woke up at seven the next morning when Tess's alarm clock started beeping. She took her turn in the bathroom—brushing her teeth, washing her face, and pulling her hair into a game-day ponytail. Back in the bedroom, she changed into her yellow Stars uniform. She was just lacing up her shoes when the phone rang. She picked up the receiver before it could ring a second time.

"Hello?"

"Yasmine?"

"Hi, Mom." Yasmine rolled her eyes at Tess, who was sitting cross-legged on the bed, brushing knots out of her waist-length hair. Part of Yasmine was embarrassed. None of the other girls' parents had called to check on them. But a bigger part of Yasmine was happy to hear her mother's voice.

"How's the tournament going?" Mrs. Madrigal asked. Yaz could picture her mother sitting at the kitchen table in one of her business suits. She always made personal calls in the morning before going to the office.

"Great! Actually, we've just been hanging out so far. But we have our first game in a few hours and a half."

"Have you had breakfast yet?"

"No." Yasmine's warm feelings were starting to drain away. She didn't need her mother to tell her to eat breakfast!

"Well, I'd better let you go do that. Listen, are you having a hard time calling me from the hotel?"

"I haven't tried yet."

"I left you a message last night asking you to call me before you went to bed. Didn't you get it?"

Yasmine looked down at the phone and, for the first time, noticed a blinking red light. "No. I didn't realize the phone took messages."

"Well, please remember to check from now on."

"Okay."

"Your dad and I also left a couple of messages for Yago, but he hasn't called back. Could you go down to his room and ask him to call home immediately? I'd like to talk to him before I go in to work."

Yasmine's mother sounded a bit impatient, which made Yasmine smile. She loved it when her parents were mad at Yago.

"Sure," Yasmine said. "I'll go find him as soon as we get off the phone."

Yasmine spoke to her father for a few minutes and then hung up. "I've got to go down to Yago's room," she announced. "Does anyone want to come with me?"

"I still have to get dressed," Tess said.

Tameka was in the bathroom.

"I'll come with you." Kyoto got up and slung her cleats over her shoulder. "I don't want you to face Yago alone."

"Safety in numbers," Yasmine said with a smile. She liked the way Kyoto seemed to understand that Yago wasn't the easiest person to live with. Lots of the Stars—like Fiona, Lacey, and Geena—were always saying that having a twin brother must be fun. *Yeah, right. About as much fun as a trip to the dentist.*

Yasmine called down to the desk and found out her brother was in room 620. Yasmine and Kyoto took the stairs up one flight.

As soon as they emerged onto the sixth floor, Yasmine could feel a slight vibration shaking the air. The throbbing of a lot of bass. "Hear that music?" Yasmine asked Kyoto. "I bet you anything it's coming from Yago's room."

Yago had recently discovered heavy metal, and he liked to play it loud. At home, Yaz's parents had made a rule that the volume on the stereo couldn't be turned above the number 4.

Kyoto raised her eyebrows but didn't comment.

Sure enough, the sound got louder as the girls got closer to room 620. As they stood outside the door, Yasmine recognized one of Yago's favorite songs. No wonder Yago hadn't answered the phone. He probably couldn't hear it ring.

Yasmine pounded on the door.

Kyoto shot her a brief smile as they waited.

Yasmine tapped her foot impatiently. After a few seconds she was tempted to just walk away. But she'd promised her mother she'd give Yago the message. Besides, Yago obviously *was* in the room. Even he wouldn't go off and leave the music blaring.

"Yago!" Yasmine pounded on the door even harder.

No answer.

"Maybe we should just leave a note," Kyoto suggested.

"Or . . ." Yasmine tried the door. She wasn't surprised when it swung open. Yago was always forgetting to lock the door at home, too.

Yasmine strode into the room—ready to tell Yago he was in trouble. But she stopped dead when she spotted a boy she didn't know. He was sitting on the bed, tying his shoes.

The boy looked up. His eyes widened slightly when he caught sight of Yasmine and Kyoto. "Oh, hi," he said. "I thought you were my roommates coming back for their gear."

"Um, no. I'm Yasmine Madrigal. Yago's sister."

"Hank." He smiled, and his green eyes crinkled up at the corners.

Yasmine smiled back. She took in Hank's curly, brown, sleep-rumpled hair, his broad mouth, and his strong-looking arms. For a moment she felt pleasantly warm all over—and then she remembered something that made her blood cool.

This appealing guy had said his name was Hank.

Yago had been talking about Hank a lot lately, ever since the lottery, when Hank had become a member of the Suns. Hank had scored two goals in the Suns' first game. Hank was teaching Yago how to juggle better. Hank played the drums.

Hank was Yago's new best friend. And that meant it didn't matter if he had made Yasmine's heart flip-flop. Any friend of Yago's had to be a milk-guzzling, video-game-playing creep.

"Where's Yago?" Yasmine demanded.

"In the shower," Hank said.

Yasmine took two steps closer to the bathroom door. "You'd better call Mom and Dad!" she hollered at the top of her lungs.

Then she dropped her voice and added, "Come on, Kyoto, let's get out of here."

She took Kyoto's hand and they fled.

TESS AND TAMEKA WANDERED DOWN TO THE lobby at about seven-forty-five.

The doors to a banquet room were open. A big banner that read WELCOME TO THE MIDWESTERN SHOOTOUT! hung above the doors. The girls went inside and discovered a table full of healthy-looking breakfast foods set up along one wall. Small tables covered with white cloths were scattered around the room.

Tess and Tameka filled plates with muffins, fruit, and scrambled eggs. By then Yasmine, Kyoto, and Yard had come down. The girls found a table and ate together. Around eight-ten they went back out to the lobby and met up with Mr. Thomas, Mrs. Essex, and the rest of the Stars.

The team piled into the van. Mr. Thomas drove about a mile down a four-lane street to the local high school where the tournament was being held. The playing fields were out behind the single-story school buildings. Faded wooden bleachers lined two sides of the field. Behind one goal was a black scoreboard, covered with an enormous MIDWESTERN SHOOTOUT banner. Team-sized clumps of kids and coaches were standing on the running track that surrounded the field.

A woman carrying a clipboard jogged up to Mr. Thomas. "You are?" she asked breathlessly.

"The Stars from Beachside, Michigan," Mr. Thomas replied.

"Umm . . . got you!" The woman made a note on her list and told the team where to line up.

"Who has our flag?" Mrs. Essex asked.

"We do!" Tess called. She helped Tameka unfurl a flag. The team had spent several evenings that week painting it. THE STARS, it read in bright yellow paint. The words were surrounded by silver stars and each team member's signature. Tess and Tameka had been elected by the team to carry it.

Marching music began to blare. The teams paraded onto the field one by one as a man with a deep voice introduced them over the loudspeaker. He sounded like a TV game show announcer.

"All the way from Stoneham in the beautiful state of Massachusetts—the Patriots!"

Tess watched as a team decked out in red, white, and blue uniforms marched onto the field.

"The pride of Beachside, Michigan—the Stars!"

Tess felt terrific as she and Tameka led their team onto the field. When the announcer asked for a round of applause, she cheered as loudly as she could.

"Do a couple of laps to warm up," Mrs. Essex called later that morning. "I want you to take it at a fast march. Let's go!"

Tess and Lacey led the group around the perimeter of the field. Then Mrs. Essex gave them a slow and complete warm-up.

By the time they finished, their opponents for the day had arrived. The Cardinals were an AYSO team from Madison, Wisconsin. They had bright red uniforms. Tess watched them stretching out in a tight circle. The Cardinals seemed confident, and several of their players were a good two inches taller than Tess.

"They look tough," Tameka commented.

Tess nodded, feeling pleased. She didn't want any easy victories this morning. She felt like running hard, working up a sweat, and *then* winning.

About five minutes before game time, Mr. Thomas called the girls together for the lineup. He put Tess in as center midfielder. *Not bad,* Tess thought. Her favorite positions were on the front line, but midfield was a close second.

And besides, the front line looked strong. Tameka was playing left wing. Rory was the center attacker. And Fiona was in as right wing. *These birds are going to have to fight,* Tess thought.

By the time the ref centered the ball, about twenty spectators had gathered in the bleachers. Most looked like kids and coaches from other teams in the tournament.

The Stars began the game in control. Rory kicked off to Fiona, who drove the ball directly into Cardinal territory. She advanced about ten yards before the Cardinal center midfielder charged in and stole the ball.

"Go, Cammie!" shouted the Cardinals' coach.

Tess paused long enough to figure out what direction Cammie was heading in, and then moved to intercept. As Tess watched Cammie drilling the ball toward her, she smiled in delight. Cammie could *move*. She dribbled like a bulldozer tearing up the ground. Tess was definitely going to need to pour on the heat to keep up with this girl.

Cammie tried to maneuver around Tess, but she let the ball get too far ahead of her. Tess stole it. She dribbled back over the halfway line before a Cardinal began to pound up from behind.

Tess pushed the ball forward to Rory. The pass was good, but as Rory fought to get control, Cammie charged. The girls battled for the ball—until Rory slipped and it went skidding into the center of the field.

Fiona quickly got control of the ball and began moving it toward the Cardinals' goal. Tess pushed herself into high gear, moving into the position Rory had left open.

"Here, Fiona!" Tess hollered.

Fiona passed outside, the ball rolling fast through the slightly uneven grass. Tess looked toward the goal and saw an opening on the left side. She planted her left foot and smashed the ball with her right instep. The ball left the ground and crashed into the net.

"Goal—Stars!" the ref called.

Tess began trotting back into her position. She couldn't hold back a smile. That play had been fun.

"Nice shot!" Fiona jogged over and gave Tess a pat on the back.

"Thanks. I feel like I could put them in all morning."

Tameka overheard. "Then we'll keep them coming your way," she promised.

The Stars spent the next ten minutes fighting their way back into scoring position—and the Cardinals were all over the Stars' front line. Tameka passed back and Tess popped in the ball over the goalkeeper's head. At the half, the Stars were leading 2 to 0.

"Nice work, girls!" Mr. Thomas said as the team came off the field.

"Looking good!" Mrs. Essex added.

Tess got some water and then went to stand with Tameka and Yasmine.

"You have the touch today," Yasmine told her.

"I know," Tess said happily. "Feels good."

Mr. Thomas left Tess in as center midfielder in the second half. She spent the next fifteen minutes running, supporting the front line during attacks and helping out with defense when the Cardinals threatened to score.

With about ten minutes left to play, Cammie made a powerful shot. But Kyoto was playing goalkeeper for the Stars. She pulled her legs together, trapped the ball with her thighs, and scooped it up.

"Coming your way, Sheila!" Kyoto hollered, rolling the ball to the defender. Sheila walloped the ball back toward the halfway mark.

Tess heard a couple of the Cardinals groan. They were starting to slow down. *Amateurs,* Tess thought as she drew on her energy reserves and dashed after the ball. She was having too much fun to worry about being tired.

She drove the ball deep into Cardinal territory, faked out a defender, and passed outside to Tameka. Tameka tapped it in. Another goal!

"That's the game!" the ref called.

The Stars won 3 to 0.

Tess was almost disappointed. She was playing so well that it seemed a shame to quit. She joined the line of Stars as they shook hands with the Cardinals. "Good game," she murmured to each of their opponents. Then Tess and Tameka walked off the field arm in arm.

Mrs. Essex was waiting for them on the sidelines. She looked excited.

"What's up?" Tess asked.

"Um, I'd like to talk to Tess privately for a moment." Mrs. Essex gave Tameka a significant look.

Tameka looked puzzled for a moment—and then laughed. "Oh! Well, I guess I'll see you later."

Mrs. Essex nodded eagerly, apparently too excited to worry about hurting Tameka's feelings.

Tameka gave Tess a curious look and then slowly moved off.

Mrs. Essex dropped her voice to a whisper. "See that woman over there?" She motioned with her chin toward a woman sitting in the front row of bleachers.

The woman looked as if she was in her twenties. She was wearing a blue skirt, a light summer sweater, and rather glamorous sunglasses. Not the kind of outfit you see on the soccer field every day. She was doodling on a clipboard she held in her lap.

Tess knew without a doubt that she'd never seen the woman before. "What about her?" she asked.

"She wants to talk to you."

"Why? Who is she?"

Mrs. Essex raised one eyebrow. "A talent scout."

"From where?"

"Well, let's go talk to her and get all the details."

"Okay," Tess said uncertainly. She followed Mrs. Essex over to the bleachers. The woman saw them coming, stood up, and offered Tess her hand.

Tess shook it, smiling hesitantly. "My coach said you wanted to talk to me?"

"That's right," the woman said smoothly. "Why don't we all just sit down for a moment?"

"Sure." Tess sat on the bench, feeling slightly light-headed. A talent scout? Was Mrs. Essex serious? This was like something out of a movie!

"My name is Alexa Smith," the woman said. Up close, she looked even younger than Tess had thought before—maybe around twenty-two.

"I'm the assistant soccer coach at Sutton Acade-

32

my," Alexa said proudly. "We're a private prep school near here and we have an outstanding soccer team."

Tess nodded numbly. Alexa didn't have to tell her about Sutton. The school was one of the most expensive in Michigan. Sutton ruled high-school soccer. Tess had heard rumors that they began training their varsity players when they were ten or eleven years old. She was always bugging her mother to take her to Sutton games—but the drive to the academy usually seemed too far.

"I'd like to invite you to come to our school this weekend and try out for our team," Alexa continued.

Tess felt as if someone had turned off her brain. She couldn't process the information she was being given.

"Me? Play for Sutton?" She barely managed to choke out the words.

"I'm inviting you to meet our head coach and work out with the team," Alexa said. "Naturally, I can't guarantee that Mary Beth will want to take you on. But our team is a little short on attackers. And the ones we *do* have are graduating this spring. I came to watch the tournament to look for anyone promising. And I must say I was impressed by your performance."

"Thanks," Tess said automatically. "I'm flattered and everything. But there's no way I could go to Sutton. The place costs megabucks. My mom could never afford it."

"The school is sometimes very generous," Alexa said. "Mary Beth is a real dynamo. If she decides she wants a girl on our team, she can pull a lot of strings to make it happen. I really think you should meet her."

"May I ask a question?"

"Of course," Alexa said. "Ask as many as you like."

"If I *do* try out and the coach *does* want me on the team, when would I start?"

"I can't say for certain," Alexa said. "But probably right away. Mary Beth wants some young talent to fill in the gaps in our front line."

"How often does the team practice?"

"Three hours a day, six days a week. That's a mixture of fitness sessions and training. Games are extra. And the team does travel quite a bit to tournaments and clinics."

Mrs. Essex raised her eyebrows. "That's pretty rigorous."

Alexa nodded. "Yes, but we have one of the best

coaching staffs in the sport. We make sure our players don't burn out mentally or physically."

Tess squinted into the sun. She felt honored that Alexa thought she was good enough to try out for the Sutton team. But the timing was less than ideal. Alexa was asking Tess to consider leaving the Stars in the middle of the season and changing schools several weeks into the term.

"I think Alexa is waiting for an answer," Mrs. Essex said gently.

Tess smiled. "I think I'll pass."

Alexa's eyes widened and her jaw dropped slightly. She looked surprised and disappointed at the same time. But she recovered quickly. "Before you make a firm decision, I'd like to talk to your parents."

"Why?"

"This is a big opportunity. I'm sure they'll want to be in on your decision."

"It's just my mom," Tess said. "And she trusts me to run my own life."

"Then there's no harm in my calling her."

Tess gave Mrs. Essex an exasperated look. Alexa was so persistent! "Okay," she agreed. "I'll give you Mom's numbers."

"All right. Tell me now. Who was that woman?" Tameka demanded.

Tess had caught up with the Stars in time to watch the next two teams play, but she hadn't wanted to talk about her offer—until her friends badgered her into it during lunch. She put her plate down on a table and slid into the seat. "You're not going to believe it."

The smell of chicken salad on whole wheat was too much for Tess to resist. She took a big bite of the sandwich.

"She's a coach for Sutton Academy," Tess mumbled with her mouth half full. She spent a few minutes telling Tameka, Kyoto, Yard, and Yaz about Alexa's offer.

"So what did you tell her?" Tameka asked.

"I told her no thanks," Tess said. "I don't want to drop off the Stars in the middle of the season. Or go to boarding school—I'd feel like I was deserting my mom."

"Sutton isn't that far from Beachside," Yard said. "You could live at home and take a bus there."

"An hour and a half each way?" Tess asked. "What time would I get home?"

"I thought your dream was to play in the Olympics," Kyoto said. "Sutton sounds like a big step in that direction. Maybe you should just go check it out."

Tess made a face. "I might have. But I don't like the way Alexa said I had to come out *this* weekend. It feels too rushed. Besides, I don't want to miss half the tournament.

"But—" Tameka started.

"But nothing," Tess said. "I made my decision, and that's that. Now let's finish lunch so we can get back to the field and check out the competition."

Tameka shrugged. "It's your life."

chapter 4

"I HOPE THEY HAVE ENOUGH PIZZA," YAZ SAID.

"Me too," Tess agreed. "I'm starving."

"Watching other people play always makes me hungry," Yard said with a laugh.

The Stars were in line for a pizza dinner. Picnic tables were set up in a grassy area at one side of the high school's main building. Several volunteers were working at tables stacked with pizza boxes, soda, salad, plates, and cups.

Tess, Yaz, Kyoto, Tameka, and Yard were in line together.

"Hey, Tess," Yard said as they waited. "Tell me more about Mia Hamm."

"What do you want to know?"

"What color hair does she have?" Yard asked.

"Brown."

"Long or short?"

"Long."

"Is she pretty?"

"Very. She's even done commercials. But why don't you ask me about Mia's *game*? The way she looks really isn't that important."

"It's important when you're trying to figure out who is signing autographs for that crowd of kids."

"Where?" Tess demanded.

Yard pointed to a cluster of kids gathered in the shade of a big tree.

"That's her, all right," Yasmine said.

"This is so totally excellent!" Tess said. "We have to get her autograph."

Yaz nodded eagerly. "Who has something she can sign?"

"Me!" Kyoto said triumphantly. "I brought my sketchbook with me. I can rip out a page for each of us." She took a small spiral-bound book out of the pocket of her shorts and began tearing out sheets.

But Yard shook her head. "Don't give me one. I'm not going over there. You make her sound like a legend. I don't want to bug her."

"That's why she's here," Tess argued.

"Maybe you could get her autograph for me."

"I'll try."

Yard went off to join Sheila and Rory. Tess, Kyoto, Yaz, and Tameka made their way over to the crowd around Mia Hamm and slowly began working their way to the front. But when they got there, Tess felt shy. She wordlessly held out the small sheet of heavy paper Kyoto had given her. She felt as if all of her blood had rushed to her head. She'd never met anyone she admired more.

"Thank you," Tess whispered when Mia handed back the paper with her signature on it. She backed away before reading what Mia had written.

Work hard and enjoy yourself, the paper said.

Tess thought the working hard part sounded good. And as for enjoying herself—well, she'd always enjoyed working hard.

chapter 5

"I THOUGHT OF A WAY TO MAKE SURE NOBODY leaves our party too early tonight," Geena told Lacey, Nicole, and Fiona as they sat at a picnic table munching pizza.

"What are you going to do?" Fiona asked. "Lock the door?"

"Very funny," Geena said. "I was thinking we should invite some of the Suns to join us."

Fiona wrinkled her freckled nose. "Sounds risky. Mr. Thomas said he was going to clamp down if he heard even a rumor that we were doing anything wrong. And I'm sure he wouldn't consider having boys in our room *right*."

"Why?" Geena asked. "It's not like they're strangers."

"I think it's a great idea," Lacey put in.

"I thought you might," Geena said with a laugh. Lacey was the most boy-crazy girl she knew. "In fact—I was hoping you might do the actual asking."

Lacey shrugged. "Sure." She twisted around in her seat, scanning the crowd. "Do you guys see any of the Suns?"

"Yago is in the food line," Geena said.

Lacey got up. "I'll be right back."

Geena smiled as she watched Lacey make her way over to Yago and his friends.

When the Stars got back to the hotel, the entire team went up to Geena's room. Yasmine felt wiped out from that day's game and the excitement of meeting Mia Hamm. She couldn't believe it was only eight o'clock. She felt as if it should be midnight.

She dropped into a chair and watched Geena and Lacey buzzing around. They ran down the hall to get ice, fiddled with the television set, and stuffed their suitcases under the beds.

"Why are you going to so much trouble?" Yaz was asking when someone knocked on the door.

"Who's that?" Tess demanded.

"You'll see!" Lacey sang out. She practically skipped over to the door and opened it.

Yaz sat up straighter when she saw her brother and some of his teammates come in. Her heart started to thud when she saw that Hank was with them. Yasmine felt like hiding. Why hadn't Geena warned her that she'd invited the Suns?

The boys immediately went over to the collection of junk food Geena had assembled. Yaz wondered if there was any way she could slip out without being noticed.

But it was too late for that. Hank saw her, smiled, and walked over.

"Hi," he said warmly, perching on the arm of her chair. "How was your day?"

The strange warm feeling that Yasmine had experienced that morning rushed back. Her face was on fire. If anything, Hank looked even more attractive this evening. His hair was damp from a recent shower, and he smelled like soap. He was wearing a gray shirt that brought out the green in his eyes. Adding to Yasmine's discomfort was the fact that Yardley, Tess, and Tameka were shooting her surprised looks.

"I had a great day," Yasmine managed to get out. "We won our game this morning. And meeting Mia Hamm was so cool."

"Definitely," Hank said.

"You talked to her?" Yasmine was surprised. Yago had no interest in women's soccer. She'd assumed his friends would feel the same way.

"Well, I tried." Hank grinned sheepishly. "I got a little tongue-tied. I mean, Mia is one of the greats."

"You think so?"

"Sure. Don't you?"

"Well . . . yeah!"

"So aren't you going to ask how our game went?" Hank gave Yaz a coy smile.

"Sure. How did it go?"

"Five minutes before the end of the game, the score was tied. I had the ball in front of the goal. Our opponent's goalkeeper was out of position."

"Easy score," Yaz said.

"A six-year-old could have made it."

"So you're a hero tonight. You put in the goal that won the game."

44

"Not exactly. . . . What happened was, I tripped on my shoelace and lost the ball to a defender on the other team. He took the ball all the way downfield and scored just as the time ran down."

Yasmine laughed out loud, relaxing a little. "Poor Hank!"

"It was pitiful. Yago was practically in tears."

Over by the food, Yago seemed to sense that he was being talked about. He grabbed a handful of corn chips and made his way over to them.

Yasmine felt herself tense up.

Yago ignored Yasmine, focusing his attention on Hank. "You don't have to be nice and talk to my loser sister," he said.

Hank's body language changed completely. The warmth seemed to drain out of him. He leaned away from Yasmine. "I thought someone should take pity on the Spazz," he said in a tone Yasmine hadn't heard before.

Yago sputtered with laughter.

Yasmine tingled with fury. How could Hank be so charming one minute—and so insulting the next? What a two-faced loser! She shot him an angry look and pushed herself out of her chair.

"Where are you going?" Hank asked.

"I have better things to do than sit around and be the object of your stupid jokes," Yasmine said coldly. She headed straight for the door. She'd been thinking about going to bed early. And now seemed like the perfect time.

"Is something wrong?" Kyoto asked, intercepting Yaz.

"Yes," Yasmine told her. "Certain people don't know how to behave at a party. I'm going to bed."

★

Tess glanced at her watch and yawned. It was 10:10, and she could feel herself fading. Yasmine and Kyoto had left ages earlier. When Tess imagined them curled up in bed, she felt jealous.

"I'm going down," Tess told Yard. The two of them had been playing chess—a game Yard was pretty good at.

Tameka looked up, surprised. She was sitting on the bed, playing hearts with Lacey, Geena, Yago, and a couple of other Suns. "Already?" she asked.

"Yeah. It's after ten. And we have a game at nine tomorrow."

"Ugh," Lacey said, rolling her eyes. "You'd think they'd give us a break and start the games at noon or something." She put down a card, and Yago moaned.

"Then they wouldn't end until midnight," Tess said. "And besides, we're here to play soccer. Not cards."

Tameka gave Tess a slightly guilty look. "Are you saying we should go to bed now?"

"Well, I think it would be a good idea," Tess said.

Geena shot Tess a fed-up look. "Tess," she said. "Some of us are interested in having a good time this weekend. If you want to go to bed, fine. But I don't see any reason why *we* have to go to sleep just because *you* want to."

Tess felt her anger flash. Why was Geena attacking her? She hadn't demanded that her teammates do anything.

"I just think staying up late on a game night is a little immature," Tess said as evenly as possible. "You can have all the slumber parties you want back home. But this weekend I think we should be concentrating on playing soccer. That's all."

"Well, thanks for your opinion," Geena said sarcastically.

"I'll be down in a few minutes," Tameka said.

"Do whatever makes you happy," Tess said,

fighting hard not to sound bugged. "Good night!" She let herself out of the room, trying to shake off her annoyance. She walked over to the elevators and pushed the Down button. *I'm sure they'll go to bed soon,* she told herself.

When she got downstairs, Kyoto and Yaz were watching television in bed.

"Your mom called," Yasmine greeted her.

"*My* mom?" Tess repeated. "Is something wrong?"

"She didn't sound upset. She just said you should call her in the morning."

chapter 6

"Did you call me?" Tess asked her mother when she reached her at home early the next morning. Yasmine was in the shower, Kyoto was getting dressed, and Tameka was still asleep.

"I sure did! I got an amazing phone call last night from a woman named Alexa Smith."

"Oh—I talked to her too."

"I know. She wants you to come out to Sutton Academy this weekend."

"I already told her I don't want to go."

"Why not?"

"I guess I don't see the point. I mean, I'm not interested in transferring to Sutton. I'd have to change schools in the middle of the year. Besides, the place costs a fortune."

"That's true, but you've told me a hundred times that Sutton is the best team in the Midwest. I expected you to be excited about the possibility of playing for them."

"Well, it's flattering and everything. But I can't just walk out on the Stars in the middle of the season."

"I guess not." Tess's mother sounded disappointed. "Alexa left me her cell phone number. If you're sure, I'll call her and tell her no thanks."

"I'm sure."

"Okay. Well, have a good game today."

"I will."

The phone call left Tess feeling unsettled. She could tell her decision had surprised her mother. Now that Tess stopped to think about it, she realized she'd shocked Mrs. Essex, too. And Alexa. And maybe even Tameka and Kyoto.

Their reactions made Tess start to question her own. What if this was her big break—and she was blowing it? She worried about her decision all through breakfast while her teammates chattered around her.

She was relieved when the team got to the field about twenty minutes before game time. She knew it was impossible to play hard and worry at the same time.

The team fell into its warm-up routine: a fast-paced march, some stretches, and then laps and ball work. By the time Mr. Thomas called for a quick team meeting, Tess was sweaty and loosened up. Her mood had improved slightly.

"Our opponent this morning is a team from Detroit called the Stingers," Mr. Thomas began. "I met their coach yesterday in a training session. She tells me her team is strong. So I want you all to look alive out there today. Okay, listen up for your positions. Geena, I'd like you to handle the goal."

Nicole and Lacey groaned as Mr. Thomas tossed Geena the multicolored goalkeeper's jersey. Tess was almost certain they looked *envious*. But that didn't make any sense. None of the Stars, except for Kyoto, were wild about playing goalkeeper. So why would they be upset?

"Tess, left defender," Mr. Thomas continued. "Tameka, right defender."

Tess and Tameka exchanged *yuck* looks. Neither

of them were wild about defense. *Oh well,* Tess thought. *At least we'll get to work together.*

"Yardley, you're in the left midfield," Mr. Thomas went on. "Fiona, center midfield. Lacey, I'd like you to take the right."

Tess saw Fiona and Lacey roll their eyes at each other. She didn't understand why they were unhappy with their positions, either. Playing the midfield was never boring. You had to decide from second to second whether to play forward or back. Fiona usually liked the mental challenge. Lacey liked to run, and midfielders did a lot of that.

"And on the front line," Mr. Thomas said. "Rory, left wing. Sheila, right wing. Nicole, you'll be our center attacker and team captain."

"Okay," Nicole said, not sounding particularly excited. When the ref called for captains on the field, she moved toward him slowly. No peppy game-day trot.

Tess frowned as she walked into position. What was wrong with the Stars? They were all acting as if they were . . . unhappy. *Did I miss something at breakfast?* she wondered.

She gave herself a mental shake when the ref

signaled the beginning of the game. *I'll find out what's going on at halftime*, she told herself.

The Stingers got the kickoff. Three long passes brought them within striking distance of the Stars' goal. A small, fast Stinger attacker was dribbling up the side of the field.

Tess ran toward her. The Stinger reacted by dribbling closer to the touchline. *Bad move*, Tess thought happily. The Stinger had just limited her maneuvering room and made Tess's job of covering her easier. Tess got between the attacker and the goal. She batted at the ball, attempting to draw it away.

The Stinger moved to the right, trying to dribble around Tess. But she tapped the ball too hard. It bounced out of bounds.

"Throw-in—Stars!" the ref called.

Tess immediately stepped over the line and scooped up the ball. The throw-in was a perfect opportunity for the Stars to take control of the game. The key was getting the ball back into play quickly—before the Stingers took their positions. Tess brought the ball behind her head and looked up the field for an open Star.

Where is everyone? Tess wondered.

Lacey, Fiona, and Sheila all should have pulled in closer so that Tess could throw the ball to them. Sheila was in position, but a Stinger was covering her.

Fiona and Lacey were way off in the center of the field. They were actually leaning up against each other!

The four players closest to Tess were all Stingers. They were all angling into position to intercept.

"Lacey, Fiona—heads up!" Tess brought the ball back and tossed it toward her teammates as hard as she could.

Fiona ran toward the ball at half speed.

The Stingers' right wing got there first. She turned the ball around and drilled it right toward Tameka. Tess stayed in position, ready to intercept if the attacker tried to pass.

The attacker faked out Tameka and drove toward the goal. Her kick was weak. But Geena reacted late, and the shot rolled gently into the net.

"Goal—Stingers!" the ref yelled.

Tess shook her head in disbelief. "What was that?" she called to her teammates. She clapped her hands loudly. "Let's get fired up! Come on, look alive!"

Yaz and Kyoto began to cheer from their spots on the bench. But the rest of the team didn't respond.

The ref centered the ball for the Stars' kickoff. Nicole passed to Rory, who sent the ball back.

Nicole began dribbling diagonally across the field. Before she'd gotten ten yards, a Stinger moved in and stole the ball. Nicole immediately stopped running and watched her dribble away with it.

"Come on, you guys!" Tess shouted. "I want to see you fight!"

That got Nicole running. But by then the Stingers had advanced the ball well into Star territory.

"Stop her, Fiona!" Tess called.

Fiona made a weak attempt to intercept. But the Stinger ran right by her.

The Stinger was a sloppy dribbler. She let the ball bounce way ahead of her. Tess put on a burst of speed. She cut in between the attacker and the ball. She whacked the ball back toward the halfway line. It landed a few feet from Nicole. But Nicole didn't seem to be paying much attention.

"Nicole, that's yours!" Tess hollered.

A Stinger got there first. She turned the ball around and began dribbling right back toward Tess.

By the substitution break Tess's voice was hoarse

from yelling encouragement to her teammates. Her patience was also shot. She marched back to the sidelines alone and impatiently waited to see what Mr. Thomas would say.

"Kyoto, go in for Lacey," the coach said. "Yaz, take over for Fiona." He paused for a moment, watching Fiona and Lacey slump down on the bench with relief. He seemed to be searching for the right words.

"Girls, I've never seen you play worse—"

"No joke!" Tess broke in, unable to control herself any longer. "You guys aren't even trying!"

There was a long pause, during which Nicole, Yard, Fiona, Lacey, Tameka, and Geena all stared at their cleats or up at the sky.

Tess groaned in frustration. "What is wrong with you guys?" she demanded.

Tameka looked up and met her gaze. "I guess we're all just tired," she said flatly. "We were up kind of late last night."

Tess thought back to the night before. She couldn't remember when Tameka had come in. She'd assumed it wasn't too late. After all, Tameka had said she'd come down in a few minutes.

The ref tooted her whistle. "Let's get this game going!"

Tameka wearily got to her feet and headed back into position.

Tess trotted after her. "How late is late?" she demanded.

"About four-thirty," Tameka said.

"You stayed up until four-thirty? In the morning?" Tess squeaked. "What were you doing all that time?"

Tameka shrugged. "Playing Truth or Dare. Talking. Hanging out."

"So you got—what? Three hours of sleep?"

"Something like that."

"How could you do that on the night before a game?" Tess asked.

"Why not?" Tameka shot back. "Hanging out last night was fun. And isn't the point of this team to make friends and have a good time?"

Tess didn't answer. Having fun and making friends was important to her, too. But she didn't understand why the Stars couldn't make friends while playing soccer instead of while playing stupid games in the middle of the night.

By the time Mr. Thomas turned the van into the hotel parking lot, Yasmine was in an awful mood. The rest of the game that morning had been a disaster. Apparently Yaz, Tess, Kyoto, Sheila, and Rory were the only Stars who had spent more than a few hours in bed the night before.

The final score was Stingers 8, Stars 0.

"I need a shower," Kyoto announced as the girls straggled across the lobby.

"I'm dying for one," Tess agreed.

"I want a nap," Tameka said.

"Too bad you didn't take one of those last night," Tess said.

Tameka just grunted in reply.

Yaz could feel Tess's aggravation bubbling just below the surface. She didn't really want to be around when Tess exploded.

"I'm going to see if the gift shop has the new *Fourteen*," Yaz said. "I'll see you guys upstairs."

★

Tess was furious with Tameka. But she was too worn out from the game to talk about it. She dragged herself over to the elevator and limped on.

She'd pushed herself hard during the game, using every ounce of energy to cover for her sleepy teammates. She'd run through cramps, ignored her thirst, and fought through fatigue.

But now that the game had been over for several hours, Tess was slowly becoming aware of how tired her body was. Her muscles were stiff. She had a painful blister on her right baby toe. And her skin felt itchy from dried sweat.

Tess wordlessly followed Kyoto and Tameka off the elevator, down the hall, and into their room.

"What's the next thing on our schedule?" Tameka asked.

"Lunch," Tess said. "And then free time until the team-spirit contest at four."

"Make sure I'm awake for the team-spirit

thing." Tameka flopped down on the bed and closed her eyes.

"We have a message." Kyoto pointed to the blinking light on the phone.

"Probably Yaz's mom," Tameka said without stirring.

"Let me know if it's for me," Kyoto said. Then she disappeared into the bathroom.

Tess heard the shower come on as she picked up the receiver. The instructions for retrieving messages were printed on a little card next to the phone. Tess carefully punched buttons in the order the card advised.

Beep. "You have one message," announced an electronic voice. *Beep.* "Hi, Tess. It's Mom," came a recorded voice. "Please call me at the office when you get back to your room. Thanks." *Beep.*

"It was my mom," Tess announced as she disconnected the call.

Tameka didn't reply. She had one arm over her eyes, and her chest was rising and falling evenly.

Tess shrugged. She dialed, wondering why her mother would call twice in one day. "Hi!" Tess said when her mother came to the phone. "Is everything okay?"

"Everything's fine. I had a long talk with Alexa this morning. And she even asked Sutton's head coach, Mary Beth, to give me a call."

"Why?"

"Well . . ." Tess heard her mother take a deep breath. "Alexa was worried when you turned down her offer without even seeing Sutton or meeting Mary Beth."

"She is so pushy!"

Mrs. Adams laughed. "She is. But I also think she might have a point. Mary Beth told me more about the academics at Sutton. Honey, you'd have a lot of special opportunities there."

"Like what?" Tess asked sullenly.

"Well, I told Mary Beth that you like math and science," Mrs. Adams said. "And she told me their science classes are extensive—physics, chemistry, astronomy, you name it. They even have a tele-scope. Oh, and they just added a class in Chinese! Wouldn't that be neat?"

"I guess," Tess admitted.

"Here's another thing that should interest you. Sutton's chess team is the state champ!"

"So you think I should go?" Tess asked.

"I'm not saying that," Mrs. Adams said. "But I

do think you should try out and meet Mary Beth. At least that way we'll all know you made an informed decision."

"But, Mom," Tess argued. "How could we afford that place?"

"Nothing's definite," Mrs. Adams said. "But Mary Beth said they'd consider giving you a full scholarship."

"You mean—I could go for free?"

"Exactly," Mrs. Adams said with a little laugh. "That's why I think this is the kind of opportunity you shouldn't turn down without careful consideration."

"Okay," Tess said with a groan. "When's the tryout?"

"Mary Beth wants you to work out with the team," Mrs. Adams said. "And since they have Sunday off, you'll have to go out there this afternoon."

"*This* afternoon?" Tess repeated. "But how am I going to get there?"

"I'll come pick you up," Mrs. Adams said.

"You will?"

"Why do you sound so surprised?"

"Because it's Saturday!" Tess said. "You never

miss a Saturday at work." Mrs. Adams sold real estate. People had time to look at houses on Saturday and Sunday. And that meant that Mrs. Adams almost always worked weekends.

"Well, I'm going to drag myself away from work for one afternoon," Mrs. Adams said. "This is a once-in-a-lifetime opportunity. Can you be ready to go at two?"

Tess considered for a moment. She felt bad about leaving the Stars in the middle of the tournament. But then again, they hadn't missed her the night before. They probably wouldn't even notice she was gone.

"Two sounds okay," Tess agreed.

"Great," Mrs. Adams said. "Oh, and one more thing. Mary Beth thought it would be a good idea if you spent some time with the other girls on the team. She suggested you spend the night in the Sutton dormitory."

"Are you going to stay too?" Tess asked.

"I wasn't planning on it," Mrs. Adams said. "I'd probably just get in the way. Why? Do you want me to stay?"

"Well, how would I get back?"

"The school will send you back to the hotel in a car tomorrow morning."

"We have a game at ten," Tess said.

"That shouldn't be a problem," Mrs. Adams said. "We'll just make sure you leave Sutton in time to make it."

"Okay. See you later."

Yasmine spent ten minutes in the hotel gift shop, browsing through the small collection of paperbacks, postcards, and T-shirts. She picked out a copy of *Fourteen* and paid for it, then flipped through the magazine as she waited for the elevator to come. When it did, she stepped in without glancing up from her reading.

"Hi, Yasmine."

Yaz lowered the magazine—and found herself face-to-face with Hank. He was wearing a baggy blue bathing suit and a damp T-shirt. His feet were shoved into untied gym shoes, and a towel was thrown over one shoulder. His hair was wet.

"I just went for a swim," he explained.

"That's nice," Yasmine said. Hank looked adorable, which annoyed her. Didn't this guy ever grow a zit on his chin or have a bad hair day? She turned her gaze to the elevator indicator, which beeped for the second floor.

"Why are you so mad at me?" Hank sounded slightly amused.

Yasmine glanced at him for a second. "I'm mad because you're rude. You called me Spazz in front of all my friends. How do you think that made me feel?"

Hank's smile faded. "I was just teasing."

"Ha, ha," Yasmine said. "I hope you haven't enrolled in clown school, because you're *not* funny."

Hank's cheeks colored slightly. "Listen to yourself," he said. "How can you talk like that and accuse *me* of being rude? You could open a rudeness academy."

"Oh, sure," Yasmine said. "Maybe I'll hire you as an instructor."

The elevator doors opened and Yasmine stomped off. *What a loser,* she thought as she started down the hall toward her room. *I can't believe I ever thought he was nice.*

But then an image floated into her mind. She remembered Hank's fading smile. He *had* been unhappy when he realized how upset she was. And didn't that prove he wasn't a complete creep?

Yasmine had to admit it was possible she had overreacted. *Maybe I'm being too hard on Hank,* she thought as she slipped her key card into the door.

TESS FELT MUCH MORE HUMAN AFTER SHE'D showered. She waited for Kyoto and Yaz to change. Then the three girls went downstairs for lunch, leaving Tameka asleep in their room.

At one-fifty, Tess went back upstairs to pick up her suitcase. Tameka stirred when she heard Tess come through the door.

"What time is it?" Tameka still sounded half-asleep.

"Almost two. You slept through lunch." Tess started hauling her overnight bag out of the closet.

"Why are you making so much noise?" Tameka asked.

"I'm getting my bag out of the closet."

"Get it later."

"I can't. I'm leaving in ten minutes."

"Where are you going?" Tameka sounded more alert now.

"To work out with the Sutton Academy team." Tess kept her tone casual. But saying the words sent a thrill through her system.

Tameka sat up, suddenly looking wide-awake. "I don't understand. I thought you didn't want to go to Sutton."

"I didn't. I mean, I don't. I mean—I promised Mom I'd go."

"Oh." Tameka watched Tess put on her jacket and pick up her suitcase. "How are you getting out there?"

"Mom's driving me."

"Really?" Tameka's worried look deepened. Tess guessed Tameka was thinking about how rarely Mrs. Adams missed a Saturday at work.

"I'll go down to the lobby with you," Tameka offered.

"You don't have to do that."

"I know." Tameka had fallen asleep with her shoes on, so she was all ready to go. "But I want to. I mean, it feels strange that you're leaving in the middle of the tournament. You're going to miss the team-spirit contest this afternoon."

"I know. But I'll be back in time for the game tomorrow." Tess opened the door and led the way into the hallway.

"Unless . . ." Tameka's voice trailed off.

Tess stabbed at the Down button, feeling a bit annoyed that her friend was making such a big deal about her going. "Unless what?" she demanded.

"Unless you like Sutton."

"Even if I do, I'll still be back tomorrow."

"So you think you might? Like Sutton, I mean."

Tess just shrugged. She wasn't sure how she felt about Sutton anymore. Alexa and Mary Beth had been aggressive in getting her to try out for the team. That was creepy—but also flattering. Obviously, soccer was taken seriously at Sutton. And Tess thought *that* might be a refreshing change.

The team-spirit contest began that afternoon at four. All twenty-four teams at the tournament were gathered in the banquet hall. The coaches were off at some workshop.

"Okay!" one of the organizers announced into a microphone. "Each team should have a stack of red construction paper, two pairs of scissors, and a roll of tape. Does everyone have their supplies?"

"Yes," the crowd rumbled back.

"Okay! You have half an hour to make the longest paper chain you possibly can. The team with the longest spirit chain wins!"

The Stars—including Geena—stared at the supplies for a long moment.

"Let's wait for Tess to get here," Geena suggested. "She'll probably know how we should tackle this."

"Tess isn't coming," Tameka said. She picked up one of the pairs of scissors. "She went out to Sutton Academy to try out for their soccer team. I'll cut."

Yard picked up the other scissors. "Cut the long way down the paper," she suggested to Tameka. "That way each link in our chain will be longer."

"Okay," Tameka agreed.

"The rest of us can tape," Geena said. "So does this mean Tess is quitting the Stars?"

"If she likes Sutton, she'll have to." Tameka started to cut the paper into long strips. "I'm hoping she hates it."

"She'll never quit," Fiona said. "The Stars are, like, the most important thing in Tess's life."

Tameka shrugged, not looking convinced.

"When is she coming back?" Geena asked.

"Tomorrow morning," Tameka said.

"So we'll know really soon," Geena reassured her. "There's no point in worrying until then."

"I guess not," Tameka admitted.

Geena picked up one of the strips and started taping it together. She was a little surprised that Tess had left in the middle of the tournament. After all, she was the team's unofficial leader. On the other hand, it *was* rather convenient that she'd be away for the evening. Now the rest of the team could have another great party without Tess nagging everyone to go to bed.

It wasn't that Geena didn't like Tess. She did. She thought Tess was pretty and smart and a fantastic soccer player. She just didn't understand why Tess had to be so *serious* all the time.

Tess stared out the window of her mother's car in disbelief. She'd known Sutton Academy would be nice—but she hadn't been prepared for *this*.

The school was located at the end of a shady street lined with houses big enough to be hotels. You couldn't see the grounds from the road because the entire property was surrounded by an eight-foot brick wall. As Tess's mother pulled the car through an elaborate iron gate, a uniformed guard stepped forward.

"May I help you?" the guard asked.

"Um, yes. We have a appointment with Mary Beth Ferguson."

"Your names?"

"Ann and Tess Adams."

The guard nodded. "I'll buzz Mary Beth and let her know you've arrived. Take this road straight for about a quarter of a mile and follow the signs to the administration building."

"Thank you." Mrs. Adam put the car in gear and nosed forward. "Pretty ritzy, huh?"

Tess nodded wordlessly. She was checking out the grounds. The gravel drive they were following was lined with sugar maples, which had turned brilliant red and yellow. The leaves blew across grass as lush as a golf course.

The grounds seemed deserted. Tess spotted only

one student, a girl who was sitting on a bench, reading a textbook.

They came to a fork in the road, marked with painted signs. Mrs. Adams turned the car toward the administration building, which turned out to be a functional-looking three-story brick building. Alexa was standing outside. She was wearing jeans and a gray Sutton sweatshirt.

Mrs. Adams pulled the car into a spot marked VISITOR. She and Tess climbed out.

Alexa came forward to meet them. "Hello, Tess! Welcome. I'm so glad you could make it." She held her hand out to Tess's mother. "You must be Ann. It's lovely to meet you."

"Thank you." Mrs. Adams put an arm around Tess's shoulders.

"Well! Mary Beth asked me to give you the grand tour. Then I'll walk you over to her office. You'll have a few minutes to chat before practice begins."

"Great." Tess forced herself to smile, even though her stomach was churning. At this point she wasn't really looking forward to meeting Mary Beth. Or to practice.

Tess had been focusing on whether *she* was interested in Sutton. But now that she had seen the place, she was beginning to wonder if she was really good enough to go to school here. What if she made a fool of herself in front of Mary Beth? What if the other girls on the team laughed at her?

The tour did nothing to set Tess at ease. Alexa showed them the classrooms first. They were equipped with oval tables, brand-new chairs, and carpets that looked as if they belonged in someone's stuffy living room.

They saw the chemistry lab, an expensive-looking telescope, and the greenhouse. Mrs. Adams occasionally asked questions, but Tess stayed quiet.

Alexa glanced at her watch as they came out of the greenhouse. "We have about twenty minutes before we should head over to Mary Beth's office. You'll see the dorms later. So why don't I show you the athletic facilities?"

"Sounds good," Tess agreed.

Alexa led the way down a pathway to a modern single-story building. She gave Tess a smile as she opened the front door. "If you end up coming to Sutton, this is where you'll spend most of your time."

"You mean, after she finishes studying," Mrs. Adams said.

"Oh, absolutely," Alexa mumbled.

Tess was overwhelmed by the Sutton gym. Alexa showed them an Olympic-sized pool, a sauna, a weight room, a fancy changing area, and a room that was designed for indoor soccer.

"This is where we practice in the winter and when the weather is nasty," Alexa said. "We'll be practicing outside today, so you'll be able to see the fields while we're working out."

"Great," Tess said.

"We also have a couple of horses," Alexa told her. "And there's a path down by the pond where you can jog or bike or in-line skate. Um, we also ice-skate out on the pond during the winter. Anyway . . . I'd better deliver you to Mary Beth."

The head coach's office was in the basement of the gym. It was small, with just enough room for a desk and three chairs. The walls were lined with trophies and plaques. Sutton had apparently won a major competition every month for the past ten years.

Mary Beth was just as tiny and tidy as her office. Tess guessed that she was about the same age as Tess's mother. She had short brown hair and piercing blue eyes. No makeup. She wore blue shorts, a tank top, and a whistle around her neck. When she saw them standing in the hallway, she waved them in.

"Thank you, Alexa," Mary Beth said shortly.

"No problem. See you at practice."

Mary Beth leaned forward and shook Mrs. Adams's hand. She asked them to sit down. Then she fixed her gaze on Tess. "So you think you're good enough to play for Sutton?"

Tess blinked in surprise. "Well, I . . . don't know."

"But you like to play soccer?"

"I love it."

"Are you any good?"

"Sure! Alexa thinks so."

"Well, we'll see what *I* think. My opinion is the one that matters around here. Why don't you go get changed?"

Tess rose uncertainly to her feet. "Okay . . ."

"The locker rooms are just down the hall."

"I know. Alexa showed me."

Mrs. Adams touched Tess's arm. "Do you want me to stick around for practice?"

Tess was terrified. Mary Beth wasn't exactly

warm and welcoming. Having her mother around would be nice. But Tess knew how anxious her mother must be to get back to Beachside and to her office.

"I'll be fine," Tess said as convincingly as possible.

"Well, okay. Why don't you give me a call when you get back to the hotel tomorrow?"

"Sure thing. See you later."

Tess gave her mother a quick kiss. She held her head up as she walked into the hallway. She didn't understand why Mary Beth had been so cold to her. Unless . . .

Was it possible that Mary Beth had already found an attacker she liked better? Maybe she'd been hoping Tess wouldn't show up. *Well, too bad,* Tess thought furiously. *I'm here and I'm going to show you how good I am—whether you like it or not!*

chapter 9

Tess pushed open the door to the locker room and was surprised to find it full of girls talking and laughing as they changed. She forced herself to smile as she walked into the room full of strangers. She put her stuff down on a bench and started pulling off her shoes.

A pretty Asian girl approached her. "Are you Tess Adams?"

"Yes."

"I'm Eve Wu, the team captain. You're going to be staying in my room tonight. Welcome to Sutton."

"Thanks." Tess laughed uneasily. Since she'd met Mary Beth, she hadn't exactly *felt* welcome.

"Did Alexa give you a tour?"

"Top to bottom. Even the greenhouse."

"What do you think?" Eve asked.

Tess pulled her cleats out of her bag and sat down to put them on. "It's very—big. And quiet. Where is everyone?"

"Home for the long weekend."

"How come you're not at home?"

"We have a competition next week, so Mary Beth scheduled practice. An hour in the morning; two hours in the afternoon."

"What's the competition?"

"I forget the name. But it should be cool. The school is going to fly us down to Atlanta on Wednesday."

"Don't you have classes?"

Eve shrugged. "Yeah. But we miss them all the time. We make up for it later. Come on—we'd better get over to the studio. Alexa hates it if we're late."

"Studio?"

"Yeah. We have an hour of aerobics and weight training before we hit the field."

"Oh." Tess tried to hide her surprise. She laced her gym shoes back up and followed Eve into the dance studio. Most of the team had already gathered inside. They were a varied group—tall, short;

long hair, short hair. But they all had two things in common: they looked fit, and they didn't fool around. As soon as Alexa started to move, they fell into her rhythm. She led them through a fast-paced routine of stretches, step aerobics, and work with light weights.

Tess was so busy trying to follow the routine that she hardly noticed the sweat dripping off her nose. She was ready to collapse by the time Alexa applauded and called out, "Nice work, everyone!"

Eve tapped Tess on the shoulder. "Ready?"

"What? Oh, sure." *You still have another hour of practice to go,* she reminded herself.

Alexa and the team headed for the field at a jog. Tess couldn't believe the Sutton team had already worked out for an hour that morning. They weren't showing any signs of fatigue.

Mary Beth was waiting for the girls on the side-lines. She greeted them with a shrill blast on her whistle.

"Let's see six!" Mary Beth called.

Obediently the team headed for the far goal line, jogging at a good pace. *Six laps?* Tess thought in disbelief. *Why? Didn't we already warm up? This is crazy. I can't run six laps now.*

When the Stars ran laps, Tess was always right up in front. Now she let Eve move off ahead of her and fell to the back of the pack. Lifting her legs was almost impossible. She felt as if someone had tied bowling balls to her ankles.

A red-faced redhead passed Tess on the left. Tess pushed herself a little harder. She didn't want to be dead last. That wasn't the way to impress Mary Beth.

As the girls rounded the field the first time, Mary Beth fell into step with the team. She ran next to the tall African American girl who was last in line. "Get your knees up, Louise. Up, up, up."

Tess overheard and tried to get her knees up higher too. She didn't want Mary Beth singling her out. By the time the girls finished the laps, Tess's heart was thumping in her chest. She'd pushed herself harder than she'd planned—and finished near the front of the group.

Alexa immediately began tossing out balls.

The pace of the practice made Tess dizzy. The Sutton team never seemed to waste a second talking, laughing—or even resting. They were in constant motion.

"Let's try the passing drill we were working on

this morning," Mary Beth said crisply. "Alexa, please play goalkeeper and take note of who is aiming well."

Without a word, the team started to move onto the field in twos. Tess felt lost. *Who am I supposed to work with?* she wondered.

"Tess, this is a simple drill," Mary Beth said. "Player A passes to Player B. Player B returns the ball. Player A shoots. Got it?"

"Sure," Tess said.

"Good," Mary Beth said. "I'll be your partner. You be Player A. I want to see how many you get in the goal."

Tess glanced over at the coach, half expecting that she was kidding. No such luck.

As the practice continued, Mary Beth stuck by Tess's side. Apparently she was taking stock of Tess's skills. The coach never cracked a smile—or even said anything to encourage Tess.

Tess couldn't remember ever being so uncomfortable on the field. But she had to admit she was playing well—especially considering that she had already played a game that morning and done aerobics for an hour. Her passes were accurate. And she put most of her shots into the goal.

Still, Tess could tell that the rest of the Sutton team had stamina and skills superior to her own. *Well, they are older,* she reassured herself.

"Okay, that's it!" Mary Beth finally announced. "Alexa, cool them down, please." She left the field without saying a word to Tess.

"March it out!" Alexa called, marching in place.

Tess mimicked Alexa's movements, wondering how she'd done. Judging from Mary Beth's attitude, not that well.

The Kalamazoo Crew—a team from Kalamazoo, Michigan—ended up winning the team-spirit contest. Yaz had to admit they deserved it.

The Stars' spirit chain had snapped in two while the organizers were measuring it. And the next event was a disaster, too. It was called the Newly Drafted Game. The organizers picked two team members and asked them questions about each other's likes and dislikes.

Yaz and Sheila had represented the Stars—and they got the lowest scores of any team.

The team had an hour of free time before dinner at six—plenty of time to take a swim or play a game. But most of the Stars were still dragging from their late night. They immediately went up to their rooms to read, watch TV, or nap.

"I can't believe everyone crashed on us," Kyoto said. She and Yaz were hanging around the lobby. "Want to get a snack in the coffee shop?"

"Nah. It's almost dinnertime."

"I saw some kids playing soccer out back," Kyoto said. "We could practice heading balls."

"Sure," Yasmine said.

The girls went upstairs long enough to retrieve a couple of balls. Then they went outside and hiked around to the back of the hotel.

Three boys were standing in a small patch of scruffy grass. Each one was juggling a ball. Yaz's steps slowed when she recognized Nathan, one of the Suns. She immediately scanned the group for Yago's dark hair but didn't see it.

The girls had almost reached the boys when Yasmine spotted another familiar figure—Hank. She hadn't noticed him earlier because his hair was hidden under a baseball cap.

Yasmine grabbed Kyoto's arm. "I'm not sure this is a good idea."

"Why not?"

Yasmine didn't know how to explain without

admitting she liked Hank. Or that she'd had a fight with him.

"What if my brother shows up?" Yasmine asked.

"Then we'll leave," Kyoto said.

"Okay," Yasmine agreed reluctantly. She didn't really feel like facing Hank, but she knew she couldn't avoid him forever. He *was* Yago's best friend. And that meant he was going to be hanging around.

"One, two, three—go!" Nathan was saying as the girls walked up. The boys began juggling. After about three seconds one of the boys accidentally let his ball drop.

"I'm out," the boy said, sounding disappointed.

Hank's ball hit the grass next.

Nathan grabbed his ball and held it high. "I win!"

"I can juggle longer than that," Kyoto called.

"Let's see you," Nathan said.

"Sure," Kyoto said. "Come on, Yaz."

Hank spun around, apparently just realizing Yasmine was there. To her surprise, he smiled. "Hi, Yaz. Come play with us. Whoever juggles the longest wins. Ready? One, two, three—go!"

Yaz started bouncing the ball on her knees. But

she was too nervous about being around Hank to really concentrate. She let her ball drop almost immediately.

Hank, Kyoto, and Nathan didn't do much better. But the third boy really got into a rhythm—he let the ball bounce from one thigh to the next over and over again.

"Go, Bill!" Nathan hollered.

Hank touched Yasmine's elbow and drew her a few steps away. "I wanted you to know. I—I decided you were right about last night. I was just showing off for Yago. I guess I feel a little uncomfortable liking his twin sister."

Yasmine felt the blood rush to her ears. Was she imagining things—or had Hank just admitted that he liked her?

"Do you forgive me?" Hank asked.

"Sure. I'm sorry I got so mad."

"You guys, get in the circle!" Kyoto called to them. "We're going to see how long we can keep the ball up if we all do it together."

"Coming!" Hank grabbed Yasmine's hand and pulled her into the circle.

Yasmine could hardly pay attention to the game at first. She kept thinking about what Hank had said. He actually liked her! She felt the need to get away by herself somewhere and absorb that amazing fact.

Having Hank so near made her self-conscious. She didn't want to look like a geek whacking the ball with her head. But on the other hand, she wanted to show Hank what a great soccer player she was.

"Okay, everyone—left feet only!" Hank announced.

The ball was heading straight for Nathan's right knee. He lurched sideways to try to get the ball with his left foot instead. He knocked into Kyoto and they both landed on the ground, giggling.

Yasmine offered Kyoto a hand up. "That was beautiful."

"Grace is my middle name!"

After playing for almost half an hour, Yasmine was hot and thirsty. But she didn't want to admit it. She was having too much fun.

"I need a swim!" Kyoto finally announced, letting the ball drop. Her face was grimy with sweat.

"Sounds good to me," Nathan said.

"Are you coming, Yaz?" Kyoto asked.

Yasmine glanced at Hank. "I guess—"

"Actually, Yaz is busy," Hank interrupted. "She'll see you at dinner."

Kyoto gave Yasmine a curious look. "Well . . . okay. See you later, then."

Yaz watched the other kids walk slowly away. She was having a hard time breathing. Maybe because all the blood in her entire body had rushed to her face. She could imagine what Kyoto would say to Tameka as soon as she got upstairs! Then Tameka would tell another Star, and so on, and so on—until the entire team knew she was "busy" with Hank.

"Why did you say I was busy?" Yaz finally managed to ask.

"Because you are!" Hank didn't seem to realize he had just told Yasmine's friends they liked each other. In fact, he looked kind of proud of himself.

"Doing what?" Yasmine asked.

"Going on our first date."

"A date? Where?"

"You'll see."

chapter 10

HANK TOOK YASMINE TO THE HOTEL COFFEE shop. He told her he had a special booth picked out and led her to one back by the kitchen. They were so far away from the other tables that even the waitress seemed to forget about them as soon as she brought their sodas.

"So . . . tell me about the Stars," Hank said.

"What do you want to know?" Yasmine felt funny talking to a boy other than Yago. But having Hank pay so much attention to her made her feel special.

"Um, who is your best friend on the team?" Hank was playing with his straw wrapper.

"I don't have just one best friend," Yasmine said. "But I've known Tameka and Tess the longest."

"Tess is the one with really long hair?"

"Right. And Tameka has braids." Yasmine started telling Hank more about her friends. She found herself talking mostly about Tess and how she focused on being the best at everything. She even told Hank about Tess's tryout at Sutton.

"I'm really scared Tess is going to transfer," Yasmine said sadly.

"But if she wants to go to the Olympics, maybe that's the best thing for her."

"I know." Yasmine took a sip of her soda. "I'm just upset because Sutton is a boarding school. If Tess goes there, I'll never get to see her. And I'll miss her like crazy."

"Why?" Hank asked. "You have lots of other friends."

"I know. But Tess is special. She's the most mature person on our team, and she helps us focus. Plus she's the most talented player we have. And the smartest—" Yaz thought of Yard. "Or at least one of the smartest. And the prettiest."

"You think Tess is the prettiest?" Hank sounded amazed.

"Yeah. Don't you think she's pretty?"

"She's okay. But you're much prettier. You're the prettiest Star of all." Hank's voice sounded sort of husky. And before Yaz knew what was happening, he leaned forward and kissed her right on the lips.

Yaz pulled her head back. She was shocked . . . and, well, pleased. Except . . . the kiss had ended so quickly. It was over before she'd had a chance to experience it.

Hank was still leaning across the table, looking at her. He was so close that Yaz could see each one of his eyelashes.

Yasmine leaned forward about an inch and lightly brushed her lips across his. He softly returned her kiss, and this time it lasted longer. Goose bumps rose all over her arms. When she sat back again, she was smiling. Now, *that* was a kiss.

★

"Why don't you guys come up to our room and hang out for a while?" Geena asked as a group of the Stars left dinner that evening.

"Sounds good," Tameka said, and the others nodded their agreement. The girls all squished into one elevator. Yasmine practically had to hold her breath until the doors opened on the seventh floor and everyone burst out.

"So where did you guys go this afternoon?" Tameka asked Yasmine and Kyoto as they started down the hall.

Kyoto motioned toward Yasmine with her head. "Ask *her*," she said in a suggestive way—as if Yasmine had some juicy story to tell.

Tameka gave Yasmine an expectant look.

Thanks a lot, Kyoto! Yasmine thought. She was still glowing from her "date" with Hank. But she hadn't told any of her friends what had happened. She knew they would tease her, and she *hated* to be teased. She got enough of that from Yago. She shrugged as casually as possible. "We practiced our juggling."

"And . . . ," Tameka prompted her.

"And nothing." Yasmine pushed into Geena's room ahead of the others.

But Lacey and Fiona had overheard. "So . . . who were you practicing juggling *with*?" Lacey asked.

Yasmine sat down on one of the beds and flicked on the TV. "Nobody important. I can't remember."

"Oh, so *Hank* wasn't there?" Fiona asked with a smirk.

Yasmine was aware that seven girls were waiting to hear what she would say. They weren't even watching the TV. She pretended she had to think back. "Yeah. Yeah, I guess Hank was there."

Kyoto sputtered with laughter. "Oh, come on, Yaz! You guys totally, like, disappeared together."

"We didn't disappear! We went to the coffee shop."

"Ooh," Fiona said. "A date!"

"It wasn't a date!" Yasmine said hotly. She couldn't believe how mean her friends were being. They were worse than Yago!

"Then what was it?" Geena asked.

"A . . . *nothing*," Yasmine said. "We were just thirsty after playing outside. So we went to get a soda. Why are you guys making a federal case out of this?"

"Because he's your first boyfriend," Tameka said gently.

"He's not my boyfriend!" Yasmine screamed.

"The lady protests too much, methinks," Nicole said with a smug smile.

"What's *that* supposed to mean?" Yasmine demanded.

"It's Shakespeare," Nicole said in this superior

I-go-to-private-school-and-you-don't way. "He was an English dramatist. It means that by *insisting* you don't like Hank, you're making it painfully obvious that you *do* like him."

"I know who Shakespeare is," Yasmine said loudly. "And trust me, he doesn't know anything about Hank and me. In case they forgot to tell you at Country Day, the dude has been dead for about five billion years!"

Someone pounded on the door.

"Who's that?" Yard asked.

Geena shrugged. "I didn't invite anyone else over." She shot a warning look at Yasmine. "Maybe it's someone who wants to complain about the yelling."

"Sor-*ree,*" Yasmine said angrily. "But if you guys would stop ganging up on me, I'd stop yelling."

Fiona opened the door. It was Yago, Nathan, and Hank.

"Mind if we come in?" Hank asked.

"No!" Fiona said, giggling. "In fact, we were just talking about you."

"All of us?" Yago demanded.

"No, just Hank."

"You were talking about *me*?" Hank said. "Saying nice things, I hope."

"Pretty nice," Fiona said.

The boys came in and immediately attacked a bag of chips that Geena had pulled out. Geena asked about the Suns' game that morning. Nathan and Yago started telling a complicated story about how they had faked out the other team's goalkeeper.

Yasmine crossed her arms and stared fixedly at the TV screen. She couldn't let her friends know that she was happy to see Hank. And, in fact, she *wasn't* happy to see him. Her friends were certain to watch every move she made around him. They were making her feel like bacteria under a microscope.

Then Yasmine had a thought that made her blood run cold. What if her friends told Yago that she'd gone on a date with Hank? Yago would never, ever let her forget it. He'd make her life miserable.

Yasmine was startled when Hank sat down *right* next to her. "What are you watching?" he asked.

Good question, Yasmine thought. Her mind had been working so fast that she hadn't even noticed what was on TV. "Um—it looks like CNN," she muttered.

Out of the corner of her eye, Yaz saw Lacey and Fiona exchange smiles. They probably thought the fact that she and Hank were sitting together proved they were a couple.

How can Hank be so stupid? Yasmine wondered. She was beginning to regret kissing such a clueless guy. Next time, she'd be much more careful.

"It *is* CNN," Hank said. "It looks like the financial news. Do you mind if I change it?"

"Why would I care?" Yasmine asked.

Hank leaned closer. "Are you mad at me again?" he whispered.

Yasmine jumped away and gave Hank a withering look. How could he be so friendly in front of all these people? If she didn't watch him, he'd probably start declaring his love in public.

She noticed that Tameka and Yard were just starting a game of cards. Without saying a word to Hank, she walked over to them.

"Can I play?"

"Sure," Tameka said. "Grab a chair."

Tameka dealt Yasmine in—but Yasmine had a hard time concentrating on the game. Even though she forced herself not to look at Hank, she was hyperaware of him.

She heard him talking to Nicole for a few minutes about the World Cup. Then he walked over and joined Yago and Nathan. She noticed he wasn't laughing, or even talking much. Did that mean she had hurt his feelings?

Yasmine felt so tense that her stomach started to hurt. She was relieved when the boys left about ten minutes later.

Hank didn't say goodbye.

Yasmine told herself she didn't care.

"I'm bored," Nicole announced about two minutes after the boys left.

"Then why don't we think of something fun to do?" Geena noticed that she was speaking in the same tone she used when her little brothers and sisters were cranky.

"Like what?" Lacey asked with a pout.

"We could watch a movie," Geena said.

Yard had the remote. She'd been flipping through channels for five minutes straight. "Nothing's on," she reported. "Cable has the same movie we saw last night. Then there's news. And some show about saving for retirement."

"Why don't we play cards?" Geena suggested.

"There are too many of us," Kyoto said.

"Want to go down to the coffee shop?" Geena asked.

"No," Yasmine said.

"We could get some balls and play out back," Geena said.

"It's already getting dark," Fiona pointed out.

That was when Geena noticed Tameka. She was sitting at the little round table, flipping through a magazine. She looked sad.

"What do you want to do, Tameka?" Geena asked.

"Um . . . I guess, nothing."

"Is something wrong?" Kyoto asked.

Tameka looked down. "I was just thinking about Tess and wondering what she's doing right now. Wondering if she likes Sutton."

The room grew quiet.

"I've been thinking about her a lot too," Yasmine admitted. "Sutton sounds so perfect for Tess. But if she left . . . well, everything would be different."

"For one thing, we'd lose a lot more games," Nicole said in a no-nonsense way. "She's one of the best players we have."

"*The* best," Yard said.

"Do you think she really might leave?" Fiona asked.

"I do," Nicole said. "Sutton is an excellent school. The governor's daughter attends. Tess would be a fool to turn down an opportunity to go there."

"They have a great chess team, too," Yard said.

"Yeah, but what about us?" Geena asked. "Tess is going to want to be with us, her team—her friends."

"Maybe," Lacey said. "But nothing is more important to Tess than soccer. And Sutton's team blows the Stars away."

"Especially lately," Yasmine said. "I think—well, I *know* Tess was pretty upset about the game this morning."

"Because we lost?" Lacey asked.

"Because you guys basically slept through the whole game!" Yasmine said with a little laugh. "I mean, it was a pitiful effort."

"Beyond pitiful," Kyoto said.

"We stayed up late one night," Geena said. "Big deal. It's not a crime."

Yasmine shook her head. "I'm not saying that. I'm just explaining why I think Tess might drop off

99

the team. She doesn't like it when we don't even *try* to do our best."

"If she *does* transfer to Sutton, when would she have to go?" Fiona asked.

"They want her immediately," Tameka said.

Yard sighed. "Hypothetically, tomorrow's game could be Tess's last as a Star."

The room was silent for a minute as everyone let that fact sink in.

"I think we should all play our best tomorrow," Yasmine said. "Sort of as a going-away present for Tess."

Everyone nodded.

"Maybe if we play really well, she'll decide to stay," Geena said.

"Maybe," Tameka said. But she didn't sound very hopeful.

Yasmine stood up. "Well, you know what Tess would say if she were here. The first step to playing well is to get a good night's sleep."

"I'm pretty tired anyway," Kyoto admitted.

Geena glanced at her watch. It was only 8:50. She thought about trying to convince her friends to stay a little later. But—as much as she hated to admit it—she was tired too.

chapter 11

After Alexa dismissed the Sutton team, Tess dragged herself back to Eve and Caroline's dorm room. Caroline was the team's goalkeeper. She had a curly mop of light blond hair that made her look like an angel.

"All the girls on the soccer team live on the same floor," Eve explained as they walked up to the second floor. The dorm looked a lot like the administration building. Tess thought it was pretty from the outside. But inside, it was dark and dank.

"That's cool," Tess said. "You get to be near all your friends."

"Right," Eve said as she unlocked their door. "Plus it's a big help during competitions. We don't have to worry that some girl on our floor will decide to have a party the night before a big game."

Caroline walked into the room and sat down on her tiny bed to take off her cleats. "It also makes it easier for Mary Beth to keep an eye on us."

Tess laughed uneasily. She didn't like the idea of Mary Beth spying on her.

Eve showed Tess the big bathroom all the girls on the floor shared. Tess took a long hot shower—her second for the day—and then changed her clothes one more time.

As she started to brush her hair, she realized how tired she was. The extra-long and extra-hard Sutton practice on top of the game that morning had completely wiped her out.

But Tess's mind was alert. She was soaking in every little detail about Sutton. Based on the next few hours, she would have to decide if she wanted to leave her old life behind and live here. That is—*if* Mary Beth decided she wanted her.

As soon as Tess was ready, Eve and Caroline took her down to the dining hall. The place looked a lot like the lunchroom at Beachside Middle School, only fancier. With most of the students away, it was practically deserted. A couple of girls Tess recognized from practice were sitting together near the windows.

Eve and Caroline went straight to an empty table that was already set. A moment later an older woman in a uniform appeared with a tray. She placed plates of food in front of Caroline and Eve. Then she gave Tess a welcoming smile. "Are you Ms. Adams?"

"Yes."

"Mary Beth told me we were having a guest tonight. I'll be right back with your plate."

"Thank you," Tess said.

Caroline made a face. "You don't have to be so polite to Patsy. She gets paid to wait on us."

Tess shrugged. All she'd done was say thank you. Since when was that so polite? She decided to change the subject.

"How did Patsy know what you wanted to eat?" Tess asked. She had noticed that Eve had a piece of chicken with her rice, carrots, and peas. Caroline had fish.

"The school has this nutritionist who works with the team," Eve explained. "She makes up a chart for each of us. Girls who need to build muscle get extra protein. Girls who are overweight get less fat. I'm allergic to fish, so I get chicken."

"Don't you ever get to pick your own food?" Tess asked.

Eve nodded. "On the first Monday of each month we get to go through the dinner line with the other kids. We can eat anything we want. Ice cream, coffee cake. We can even get seconds."

"I always have, like, four bananas," Caroline confessed. "I love them."

"You're not allowed to have a banana if you want one?" Tess asked. "I mean, bananas are good for you. Potassium, fruit."

"Fattening fruit," Caroline said with a shrug.

Patsy came back with a plate for Tess—which was identical to Caroline's. Tess wasn't crazy about fish. *If I come here, I'm telling the nutritionist I'm allergic to seafood,* she decided. The girls started to eat.

"So, do you guys ever cheat on your diets?" Tess asked.

"No," Eve said promptly.

Caroline shook her head.

"You never hide cookies in your room?" Tess asked.

"The menus are designed to help us play our best," Eve told her. "Why would we want to cheat?"

Tess kind of understood what Eve meant. But she also thought she would miss eating *what* she wanted *when* she wanted.

"So what else are you guys interested in?" Tess asked.

Eve and Caroline looked at her blankly.

Tess tried again. "Are you in any other clubs at school? I play chess, and I hear the Sutton team is great."

"You couldn't be on the chess team and play soccer," Eve said with a little shake of her head.

"Why not?"

"Soccer eats up a lot of time," Eve said. "Two practices a day, six days a week. That's a total of eighteen hours, not even counting games."

"Plus, the academics here are pretty intense," Caroline put in. "I spend most of my free time studying."

"It doesn't sound as if you have much time for fun," Tess said.

"I have fun while I'm playing," Eve said, a bit smugly. "If you don't think playing hard is fun, you probably won't like it here. Oh good. Here's dessert."

"Thank you," Tess murmured self-consciously as Patsy put a bowl in front of her. Inside was a tiny scoop of fruit ice. *Ice cream would probably be too much fun,* Tess thought.

★

Someone knocked on Eve and Caroline's door early the next morning. The girls were still in bed. Tess was sleeping in a cot near the door, so she opened it.

Alexa poked her head into the room. "Good morning, girls," she said. "Tess, hurry up and get dressed. Mary Beth is waiting for you in her office."

Tess felt her stomach twisting as she got up and pulled on her jeans and T-shirt. She was about to find out if Mary Beth thought she was good enough to be on the Sutton team.

"Do you want me to walk you over to the gym?" Eve offered when Tess came back from washing up in the bathroom.

"Thanks," Tess said. "But I can find it. You guys should sleep in. This is your one morning off, right?"

"Right."

"So sleep. It's only seven-thirty."

"Good luck," Caroline said without sitting up. "I hope you made it."

"Thanks," Tess said. She picked up her overnight bag and let herself out. She was glad Eve hadn't insisted on coming with her. Now she didn't have to worry about anyone overhearing when Mary Beth rejected her.

The door to the head coach's office was open. Mary Beth was sitting at her desk, drinking a cup of coffee and talking on the phone.

"I'm going to be a while," Mary Beth said when she saw Tess. "Go over to the dining room and grab some breakfast. Be back here in fifteen minutes."

Yes, ma'am, Tess thought. "Okay," she said out loud.

Tess glanced at her watch. It was 7:50. The Stars' game that morning started at ten. The drive back to the hotel would take thirty minutes, tops. *I have plenty of time,* Tess thought.

But when she got back to Mary Beth's office, Alexa was inside. She and Mary Beth were hashing out some complicated travel schedule for the team. Tess had to wait in the hallway until they finished.

Tess's watch read 8:20 when Alexa finally stepped out of the office and told Tess to go in.

"I spoke to your teacher, Mr. Hollinsworth, this morning," Mary Beth announced as soon as Tess had perched on the edge of a seat.

"You did? But it's Sunday."

"I called him at home," Mary Beth explained. "And he urged me to offer you a full scholarship. He said you are a very bright girl who could benefit from a superior Sutton education. And I'm convinced that you'd be a great addition to our team. *Especially* after we get you in top-notch condition."

"Thank you," Tess said.

"Take one week to think about it," Mary Beth said.

"I don't need a week."

"No?"

No, and I don't want one either, Tess thought. *That would just give me seven whole days to chicken out.*

"I'd love to come," Tess told Mary Beth, sounding much more certain than she felt. *Why shouldn't you be certain?* Tess asked herself. Unlike the Stars, Mary Beth took soccer seriously. What more did she need to know?

"Good," Mary Beth said. "I'll call your mother

and work out the details. Hopefully, you can be back here by the beginning of next week. We have a lot of ground to cover."

Mary Beth reached out and shook Tess's hand. "I've arranged for a car to take you back to the tournament. You can wait for it outside of the administration building. Goodbye."

Tess had a lot of questions she wanted to ask. But Mary Beth had already picked up the phone. Tess got up. "Well, see you soon," she said.

Mary Beth nodded and gave Tess a brief smile.

Tess walked up to the front of the administration building. There was no car, so she sat down on a bench to wait. Five minutes passed. Then ten. Then fifteen. Tess looked at her watch: 8:45. If the car came right away, she still wouldn't get back to the hotel until 9:15. That left just enough time to change into her uniform and be ready when the team headed out at 9:30.

The driver forgot about me, Tess decided. All she could think to do was go back to Mary Beth's office and ask for her help.

Tess double-timed it back to the basement of the gym. Even from a distance she could see that Mary Beth's office door was closed.

Now what? she wondered. A quick glance at her watch revealed that it was 8:50. Tess was starting to feel panicky. If the car didn't show up—and soon—the Stars would leave the hotel without her.

I don't want to miss my last game with the Stars, Tess thought. She felt almost teary. She could only think of one other place to look for Mary Beth: the dining room. She took off at a run.

The dining room was completely deserted—at least Tess thought so until Patsy came out of the kitchen.

"Ms. Adams . . . Is something wrong?"

"I have to find Mary Beth," Tess said breathlessly. "Have you seen her?"

"No, but Alexa is here."

"Where?"

Patsy motioned Tess into the industrial-sized kitchen. Alexa was standing at a stainless steel counter, eating a bowl of oatmeal and fruit. Once she understood the problem, she picked up her cell phone and made a call. She had a brief conversation and then turned off the phone.

"Mary Beth ordered the car for nine o'clock," Alexa said.

Tess glanced at her watch. "I've got to go!

Thanks for your help." She ran all the way back to the administration building. A big black car was idling in front. An older man was leaning against the hood, smoking a cigarette.

"You Tess?" the man asked.

"Yes. And I'm late. Can we go right now, please?"

"Sure, kid." The man dropped his cigarette, crushed it out, picked up the butt, and pocketed it. "You can ride up front with me," he said, unlocking the door. "By the way, I'm Bob."

"Hi, Bob," Tess said as she scrambled into the front passenger seat. She was hoping Bob liked to drive fast. If he didn't, she was never going to make the game.

chapter 12

YASMINE PUSHED HER SCRAMBLED EGGS TO THE left of her plate. Then to the right. Then back to the left. She was feeling too miserable to eat—maybe because she had been up half the night worrying about Hank.

She kept replaying the events of the night before in her mind, wondering why she had been so mean. She was ashamed of herself.

"It's nine-twenty," Tameka said. "I wonder what happened to Tess. She's going to miss the game."

"She still has ten minutes," Kyoto said. "I've got to go upstairs and grab a ponytail holder. Do you guys want anything from our room?"

Tameka stood up. "I'll come with you. I need to get my cleats. You coming, Yaz?"

"No, I'm all set. I'll meet you in the lobby."

Yasmine was chewing one tiny bite of eggs when Lacey and Fiona sat down at her table.

"You look bummed out," Fiona said. "What's wrong?"

"Nothing," Yasmine said warily. She didn't want Lacey and Fiona to start teasing her again.

"Listen," Lacey said. "I wanted to tell you I'm sorry about last night. We shouldn't have given you such a hard time about Hank. I just thought you had a boyfriend, and I thought it was cool. I didn't mean to upset you."

Fiona nodded. "Being teased about liking someone you don't like is beyond annoying."

"But you guys were right," Yaz whispered. "I *do* like him."

"So why deny it?" Lacey asked.

"Because—well, I guess I'm embarrassed."

Lacey shook her head and smiled. "Embarrassed about what? You're almost thirteen. You're *supposed* to like boys. It's, like, the birds and the bees. Biological destiny. Cool stuff."

"Especially cool if the guy you like likes you back," Fiona added.

"You're thinking about Josh, aren't you?" Yasmine asked.

"Yeah . . . ," Fiona said. "But Josh is only my sort-of boyfriend. We're not as serious as Lacey and Cole."

Lacey shrugged, not denying it.

"Do you and Cole ever fight?" Yasmine asked Lacey.

"Not *fight*-fight," Lacey said. "But sometimes we get mad at each other. Like, if I don't return a phone call right away or something."

"So what do you do?" Yasmine asked.

"Same thing you'd do with a girlfriend," Lacey said. "Apologize."

"Just like that?"

"Of course, just like that." Lacey made a don't-be-stupid face. "Boys are people too, you know. Why? Did you and Hank have a fight?"

"Well, I wasn't exactly *friendly* to him last night."

"So go find him and tell him you're sorry. You'll feel much better."

"Okay . . . ," Yasmine said uncertainly.

"And hurry up," Fiona put in. "We're leaving in about five minutes."

Yasmine stood up and scanned the banquet room. She didn't see Hank, so she headed out to the lobby. He wasn't in the gift shop. Or hanging around the front desk. Or outside under the canopy.

But then Yasmine thought she spotted a familiar baseball cap inside the coffee shop. *Please let him be alone,* she thought. She slipped inside the shop.

Hank was sitting at one of the front booths. He had an enormous glass of soda in front of him. He was laughing, which made Yasmine think he probably wasn't alone. Some of his friends must be sitting on the other side of the booth.

Yasmine couldn't see them. But she heard Yago's voice. "Okay, Hank, your turn, buddy-boy!"

Hank gulped down about half his soda. Then he started burping the national anthem! He got all the way to "what so proudly we hailed" before he ran out of air.

Yasmine froze, too grossed out to move. Did she really want people to think she liked this guy? What if he started burping songs at her friends?

She shuddered and backed out of the coffee shop practically on tiptoe. *Forget Hank,* she told herself when she was safely back in the lobby. *In fact, forget boys—at least until you're twenty-one. Or thirty-one.*

Yasmine spotted the Stars over by the main door. She hurried over to Tameka and Kyoto.

"Where have you been?" Tameka asked.

"Nowhere. Did Tess get back?"

"Not yet. Dad says we can only give her two more minutes. I'm worried. Being late is not her style."

★

Tess stared glumly at the line of cars stretching ahead as far as she could see. "Where did all this traffic come from?" she asked.

Bob shrugged. "Must be some construction up ahead." He beeped his horn and inched the car forward.

Tess glanced at her watch. 9:32.

"You might as well relax," she told Bob with a sigh. "I missed my ride to the field. I'm never going to get to my game now." *And I'm never going to get to play as a Star again,* she added to herself. She felt incredibly sad.

★

Yasmine was disappointed when Mr. Thomas finally decided the team had to leave without Tess. How could they show her they were serious about soccer if she wasn't even at the game? Yaz was sure Tess's absence was a bad sign. Maybe she was never coming back.

Mrs. Essex stayed behind to wait for her. She and Tess would take a taxi to the game—*if* she ever showed up.

At the field, the Stars had just enough time to warm up. As soon as they had jogged a few quick laps and stretched out, Mr. Thomas began running through the lineup.

Tameka and Yasmine kept looking toward the parking lot. *Come on, Tess,* Yasmine thought. She wasn't really paying much attention to the coach until she heard Mr. Thomas say her name.

"Yasmine, you'll be our center attacker and team captain for the day."

"Can I say something?" Yasmine asked.

"Hurry up. It's almost time to start."

Yasmine cleared her throat and looked around at her teammates. "Yesterday we agreed to play our best today for Tess. I don't think that should change just because she isn't here."

She was relieved when the others nodded. *At least we'll be able to tell Tess we played hard,* she thought. *I just hope she still cares.*

★

It was almost ten-thirty by the time Tess and Mrs. Essex arrived at the Stars' game.

"What's the score?" Tess asked as they joined Mr. Thomas and Yard on the sidelines.

Yard gave Tess a big smile. "Welcome back! What happened to you?"

"Traffic was brutal."

Mr. Thomas gave her a pat on the back. "Well, we're glad you're here now."

Tess was about to ask who was winning when she was distracted by the action on the field.

Geena was running with the ball. She crossed the halfway line. A girl from the other team leaped in front of her. The ball hit the opponent's shin guards and went skittering into the center of the field.

"I've got it!" Tameka put on a burst of speed and reached the ball first. She stopped the ball between her feet and then kicked it forward to Yaz.

Yaz dribbled toward the goal, moving at a fast pace.

"Go, Stars!" Tess hollered. She was amazed to see that Lacey and Nicole—who were also playing on the front line—were in perfect position.

Nicole was open. She ran up along Yaz's side. "Send it here!"

Yasmine passed.

Nicole's foot met the ball squarely, sending it straight into the net.

"Goal—Stars!" the ref hollered.

Nicole, Yaz, and Lacey exchanged hugs and high fives. Now Tess knew who was in the lead without being told. The Stars looked unstoppable.

Tess turned to Yard. "What a great play!"

"We've been playing like World Cup finalists all morning," Yard said proudly. "I even made a decent pass in the first half."

"Good for you! But I'm confused. I was expecting half-dead party zombies. What happened? Did you guys get busted for making too much noise?"

"Nope, we had a voluntary early lights-out." Yard's expression grew more serious. "We wanted to play well today for you. Everyone's worried you're going to take off for Sutton."

"Really?" Tess's chest went all achy. "That's so sweet."

Yard shrugged. "How did it go, anyway?"

"Pretty good."

"So are you going to transfer?"

Tess was distracted by the sound of the ref's voice. "Substitution break!" she hollered. "Take two!"

The team started to come off the field. Yasmine and Tameka began to trot when they saw Tess.

"Nice play, you guys!" Tess called to them.

"Thanks!"

"We waited forever for you this morning. What happened?"

Fiona and Lacey were right behind them. "How did it go, Tess?"

"Are you going to school with the rich and famous?" Nicole asked as she joined the group.

"Well, I . . ."

Tess looked around at the Stars. They were all waiting for her answer. Even Mr. Thomas and Mrs. Essex.

For the first time that day, Tess felt as if she was with people who really cared about her. The Stars might not be one of the five best soccer teams in the country, but they were a *team*. Her team. How could she tell them she was leaving to go play for Mary Beth? *Just keep it simple,* Tess told herself. She took a deep breath.

"No," Tess said. "I decided it's better for me to stay here."

Tameka's face lit up. "Are you serious?"

"Totally serious."

"But what about the Olympics?" Yasmine asked.

"I still want to go," Tess said firmly. "But that's not *all* I want to do in life. Having fun is important too. And you guys are *much* more fun than those chicks at Sutton."

"Line up!" the ref called.

"Yikes," Mr. Thomas said. "Are two minutes up already? Tess, why don't you go in for Lacey?"

"Right wing," Lacey said.

"Thanks." Tess gave her a smile and jogged out onto the field.

Tameka fell into step beside her. "I still can't believe you're staying."

Tess laughed. "Me neither! But it definitely feels right."

chapter 13

DURING FREE TIME THAT AFTERNOON, KYOTO and Yasmine took a couple of balls outside.

"I wonder if any of the Suns will be out," Kyoto said as they made their way around the building.

"I hope not." Yasmine made a face. But when they got closer to the grassy area and she saw that it was empty, her heart sank. She had secretly been hoping to see Hank.

Yasmine never would have admitted it to any of her friends, but she missed Hank. Well, not *all* of him. The burping part she could definitely do without. But the kissing part—that was another story.

★

Tess called her mother right after the game that afternoon. Mrs. Adams agreed with Tess's decision. She promised to call Mary Beth and break the news. That left Tess free to enjoy the last evening of the tournament. Dinner was served in the banquet room. While the kids and coaches ate, the organizers passed out a silly award to every team.

The Suns won the Hungriest Team award. It turned out that they had spent more than a hundred dollars on room service.

The Stars won the Most Unpredictable Team award. To prove the team deserved the title, the organizers showed video clips from the Stars' game that morning. They looked like pros—covering the field, playing their positions, dribbling with ease.

Then came some footage from the day before. The first shot was of Geena yawning broadly with her eyes closed. The ball bounced into the picture—right in front of Geena's face. A second later she opened her eyes. There was no sign that she realized she had missed anything.

Tess didn't think about Sutton except once—when she went back for her second piece of cake.

Poor Caroline and Eve, she thought, licking chocolate off her fingers.

Some of the teams took off for home right after the banquet. But the kids from Beachside weren't due to check out until the next morning.

"I have an idea," Tess said as the Stars waited by the elevator after dinner. "Let's party in *my* room tonight."

Geena raised her eyebrows. "Are you serious?"

"Why not?" Tess said. "We don't have a game tomorrow. Or school. We might as well have some fun."

"So the aerobic torture session is finally over," Tess said later that evening. She was telling Geena and the rest of the Stars about her adventures at Sutton Academy. "I'm soaked in sweat—even my ponytail holder is sopping. And now it's time for practice to begin!"

"You must have wanted to pass out," Tameka said with a laugh.

"I did—but wait. That's not the worst part. Next comes a little jog—"

"What was that?" Fiona asked. "Your warm-up?"

"Exactly," Tess said. "As if we weren't warm enough after an hour's worth of aerobics. So after the jog, we're supposed to run some drills. And my partner is . . . Mary Beth!"

"The coach?" Yasmine asked.

"You bet. So we're running drills. And she has one eye on the ball and, like, one on my technique!"

"Get out of town!" Nicole said.

Tess held up her hands. "All true."

Geena glanced at the TV. The Late Show was on. That meant it was almost midnight. And the party didn't show any sign of slowing down. Even Yasmine—who had looked positively weepy during dinner—was laughing at Tess's stories.

Nicole leaned over to Geena. "Are you having a good time?"

"Absolutely. This is the party I've been wanting all weekend!"

★

"Come on!" Tameka urged her friends the next morning. "Dad said everyone is waiting for us."

"Don't yell at me," Tess said as she stooped down to peer under the bed. "You were the one who turned off the alarm and let us all oversleep."

"It wasn't me," Tameka said. "It was Kyoto."

Kyoto came out of the bathroom. "Whose toothbrush is this?"

"Mine," Yasmine said. She took the toothbrush from Kyoto and stuck it in the breast pocket of her jeans jacket. There was no way she was going to open up her suitcase again. She'd already done that three times.

"Come on!" Tameka said again. "I'll go push the button for the elevator."

Yasmine followed Tameka into the hallway, dragging her suitcase. She'd only gotten four hours of sleep—and she was way too tired to pick up the heavy bag. Besides, Yasmine was still bummed out about Hank. That made her feel totally blah.

Bing. The elevator doors opened and Yasmine pulled her suitcase in. It wasn't until the doors were sliding shut that she realized Kyoto, Tess, and Tameka were still standing in the hallway.

"Aren't you guys getting in?" Yasmine called. She tried to stick her hand in the door but chickened out at the last second. The door closed and the elevator started to move. "What's up with them?" Yasmine muttered to herself.

"I think they wanted to give us some time alone."

Yasmine spun around. Hank was standing in the corner of the elevator, wearing his baseball cap and looking as adorable as ever. She had been aware that *someone* else was in the elevator. But she'd been too out of it to notice who.

Before Yasmine could recover, Hank reached forward and hit the big red Stop button. The elevator lurched to a standstill. Somewhere far away, an alarm started to wail.

"What are you doing?" Yasmine demanded.

Hank smiled. "We only get along when we're alone. So I want to make sure nobody interrupts us."

Yasmine couldn't help smiling back. "I think someone is going to come looking for us pretty soon."

"Why? Because your friends will miss you?"

"No, silly. The alarm."

"I think we have a few minutes."

"I was looking for you yesterday," Yasmine said. "I wanted to say I was sorry for the way I acted Saturday night. Before you guys came over, my friends were teasing me pretty bad. I just couldn't take it."

"I guess that makes us even," Hank said.

"Right. We both acted like jerks."

Hank laughed. But he also looked a little sad. "Do you think we can be friends?" he asked.

Yasmine considered. "Only if we keep the fact that we're friends secret. At least until the rest of our friends get too old to tease us. Especially Yago."

"How long do you think that will take?" Hank asked.

"Ten years for my friends. But Yago is a slow learner. We'd better give him fifty."

"That's a long time to wait." Hank stepped closer. "Could I have something to make the waiting easier?"

Yasmine could hardly breathe—which made talking nearly impossible. So she just nodded.

Hank ducked his head and pressed his warm lips against hers.

At that second a loud voice began shouting from outside the elevator door. "Hank? Are you in there, buddy? Don't worry, man, help is on the way. We're going to save you!"

Yasmine groaned and stepped away from Hank. "My brother always has to ruin everything," she whispered. She wasn't sure how well Yago could hear her. She could hear *him* well enough.

"He's not that bad," Hank said. He reached out

and pulled the Stop button out. The alarm stopped and the elevator slid into motion, finishing its journey to lobby level.

"See you in ten years," Hank whispered just as the doors began to open.

Yasmine could see a bunch of her teammates clustered just outside the elevator doors. "See you around," she said.

Soccer Tips from AYSO™

THE THROW-IN

The throw-in is the only time in a soccer game when a player other than the goalkeeper can use her hands. During a game, if the ball crosses the touchline, the referee stops the action. The game is restarted when the ball is thrown in by a player from the team that did *not* touch the ball last.

Key Elements of a Throw-in
- The ball must be thrown in from the place where it last left the field.
- The thrower must face the field, and both feet must remain on or behind the touchline.
- The ball must be thrown with both hands from behind and over the head. The ball can generally be thrown farther with one hand than with two, which is why the one-handed throw is illegal.

Essential Facts About the Throw-in
- The ball is in play as soon as it is released from the thrower's hands and enters the field of play.
- The thrower may not play the ball a second time in succession without incurring the penalty of an indirect free kick for the opposing team.
- If the ball is improperly thrown in, it must be retaken by a member of the opposing team.

- A goal may not be scored directly from a throw-in.
- As long as it crosses into the field of play, there is no minimum distance the ball must be thrown.

AYSO Soccer Definitions

Attacker: The player in control of the ball, attempting to score a goal. Attackers need speed, power, good ball control, and accurate aim. Sometimes referred to as forward.

AYSO: American Youth Soccer Organization, a nationwide organization guided by five principles:

1. Everyone plays
2. Balanced teams
3. Open registration
4. Positive coaching
5. Good sportsmanship

Cleats: Projections on the soles of soccer shoes that provide support and a better grip on the soccer field.

Defender: The player whose primary duty is to prevent the opposing team from getting a good shot at the goal. Defenders need sufficient speed to cover opposing players, good tackling skills, and determination to win control of the ball.

Dribbling: Moving the ball along the ground by a series of short taps with one or both feet.

Goal: Scored when the entire ball crosses the line between the goalposts and underneath the crossbar.

Goalkeeper: The last line of defense. The

goalkeeper is the only player who can use her hands during play within the penalty area.

Halftime: A five- to ten-minute break in the middle of a game.

Halfway line: A line that marks the middle of the field.

Midfielder: The player who supports the attack on the goal with accurate passes and hustles to get back to help the defense. Positioned in the middle of the field, she must have stamina for continuous running.

Open: A player who is not being marked or covered by a member of the opposing team is open.

Passing: Kicking the ball to a teammate.

Referee: An official who ensures the safety of all the players by enforcing the rules during a game.

Save: The prevention of an attempted goal, usually by the goalkeeper.

Scrimmage: A practice game.

Short-sided: A short-sided game is played with fewer than eleven players per team.

Substitution break: A quick break during which the coaches can put in new players and the players can grab a sip of water. Substitution breaks come one quarter and three quarters of the way through a game.

Throw-in: When the ball crosses the touchline, it is thrown back onto the field by a member of the team that did not touch the ball last. The thrower must keep both feet on or behind the touchline and throw the ball over her head.

Touchlines: Out-of-bounds lines that run along the long edges of the field.

Trapping: Gaining control of the ball using feet, thighs, or chest.